Worthy of Redemption

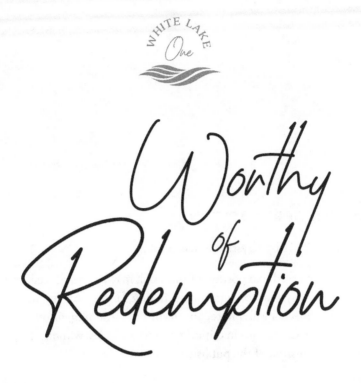

WHITE LAKE
One

Worthy of Redemption

KRYSTINA RENAE RANKIN

QUIRKY BULLPEN PRESS

WORTHY OF REDEMPTION

Cover and interior design by Roseanna White Designs
Cover images from Shutterstock.com

ISBN: 978-1734571-50-9

Dedicated to my niece Kennady,
May you grow up to be strong, compassionate,
and know you are beautiful inside and out.
I pray when you read this someday
you will see that dreams come true!
I love you!

Prologue

May, ten years ago

What she wouldn't give to be anywhere but here. Ashlynn stood in the foyer, house party in full swing around her, and wished she could disappear into the paneled walls behind her.

"I thought you said this was going to be a small party," Ashlynn said to her best friend, Victoria, as a boy she had never seen before ran past.

"I think some of the seniors from Pine Grove decided to bring their graduation party here, too." Victoria shrugged.

"I'm really not sure this is how I want to spend my high school graduation night."

Victoria turned to her, bottom lip out. "Come on, Ash. This is one of the last nights we have together before you abandon me to go to your fancy Christian school in Colorado."

Ashlynn sighed. Victoria's guilt trip was the main reason she was even at this party. She knew Denver Christian University was a much better fit than the University of Texas, even if it was further away. Convincing Victoria of that, however, had been more difficult.

"Come on, let's go find people we know!" Victoria grabbed Ashlynn's arm and dragged her out of the house to the large field behind it.

The smell of beer mixed with cigarette smoke, hay, and freshly mowed grass assaulted her nose as Ashlynn walked toward the large barn, where apparently even more people were gathered. This was people's idea of fun?

"Courtney!" Victoria yelled, waving.

"Tori!" The redheaded girl ran over and hugged Victoria, then cast a glance her way. "Oh, and Ashlynn! I can't believe I'm seeing you here. I figured you'd be with all the other holy rollers at the church party tonight."

She handed each of them a red cup. Ashlynn took hers, trying not to slosh the liquid inside.

"Victoria and I always said we'd celebrate high school graduation together, so here I am." Ashlynn offered a bright smile while looking around for a place to throw away whatever concoction she had just been given.

Victoria elbowed her playfully, then leaned in toward Courtney. "Did you see who Andrew brought with him?"

Ashlynn listened politely, then spotted a card table in the corner of the barn with safer-looking drinks. "I'll be right back."

Making her way through the throng of people, most of whom she had never seen before, Ashlynn finally made it to the table and grabbed a Diet Coke.

"Do my eyes deceive me, or is Ashlynn Wilson actually at a party?" A smooth, baritone voice said from behind her.

It was Heath, Victoria's bad-influence boyfriend. Ashlynn turned, trying not to let her face betray her true feelings. "Well, it's good to see you, too, Heath. Victoria said she told you she and I were coming together."

"Oh, she did. I just never thought she would actually convince you to show up. Shouldn't you be off praying somewhere or something?"

Her hand tightened around the Diet Coke. "Why are you at the boring drink table? Shouldn't you be at the keg or downing whatever concoction is in those red cups?"

"Nope. There's a strict no-drinking policy for anyone underage on the football team at Texas."

"Huh, never thought something like a policy would stop Heath Lancaster from doing whatever he wanted."

He opened his hands wide. "I like having fun as much as the next guy, but drinking cheap beer or trashcan punch is not worth my football career. I don't really like the stuff, anyway." He grabbed a Dr. Pepper. "I'm usually the designated driver at these parties."

"Heath! Ashlynn! My two favorite people are both here, and talking to each other." Victoria giggled, dancing up from behind. "See, I knew you guys could get along." The alcohol in her drink was already evident.

"I wouldn't go that far, Tori. We tolerate each other at best." Heath said slinging his arm around Victoria's shoulders.

"Thanks for at least trying, then." Victoria giggled again and buried her head in Heath's shoulder.

Ashlynn rolled her eyes. She received lectures almost daily from her best friend about giving Heath more of a chance, but apparently the same was not expected of him. She sighed as she followed them both back over to the other side of the barn, where Courtney and some of the other cheerleaders stood.

It felt like hours later, maybe it was, when Ashlynn followed Victoria back into the main house yet again. But this time she made her way to the food table while Victoria headed to talk to yet another group of people Ashlynn had never met.

"Food for thought?" The voice came from behind her.

She turned to see Heath holding up a bowl of chips. She gave him a weak smile and scooped out some chips onto her plate. "Thanks."

"You don't look like you're having a particularly good time," Heath said in a surprisingly genuine tone.

"Honestly, I'm trying to figure out why Victoria even wanted me to come here with her," Ashlynn blurted, then remembered who she was talking to.

"You mean why invite you if all she was going to do was ignore you all night?"

She just shrugged as she dipped a chip into the salsa.

"That's Tori." He said, ignoring her glare. "I rarely see her at these parties, either."

"Why do you keep coming with her, then?"

"Someone has to look after her. She usually drinks too much to get herself home, and so do most of her friends. I don't mind the crowds, and usually my friends are here, so it's not that big of a deal. Plus, it helps me keep up the "bad boy image" I've got going." He winked.

"You mean you aren't really the partying, rules are meant to be broken type?" The idea was surprising, could she and Heath both actually have Victoria's best interests at heart?

"I was a couple of years ago. It's just not as appealing as it used to be."

She looked at her watch, then blinked. She needed to be home in half an hour. "I have a curfew. I better go let her know we're leaving."

But telling Victoria did not go well.

"What? We just got here!" her friend yelled.

"Victoria, we've been here for over three hours. And I have a curfew. I told you that!"

"Come on, Ash! Surely your parents won't care if you're a little late. We're high school graduates. Adults! What's the worst they can do?"

"They can refuse to pay for college, that's what." Her parents

10

were already unsure about her going off to "God school" convinced that her decision to become a Christian was just some phase she was going through. They were trying hard to be supportive though and she did not want to give them a reason to change their minds.

"Well, then you'll have to go to UT with me! See, it's the perfect solution." Victoria grinned, her words starting to slur.

"Victoria." Ashlynn pulled her aside. "We are not having this conversation here. You said if I came with you we would leave when I needed to. We're leaving."

"But I'm not ready to leave," Victoria said in a singsong voice. "Courtney will take me home, right, Court?"

"Sure will, Tori!" Courtney's words slurred worse than Victoria's.

Ashlynn crossed her arms and stared at Victoria. "Courtney can barely stand up, and I am not letting you get in a car with her. Courtney, come on. I can drive you home, too." A lump settled in her throat. She did not know if she more angry at being completing ignored, or concerned how completely different of a person Victoria seemed to be when she was here.

Victoria staggered back and tossed her hair. "Yeah, that's not happening. Sorry, Ash, but if you want to be boring and leave, then leave. We're staying here."

With that, Victoria grabbed Courtney's hand and headed outside, back toward the barn.

"Hey, I'll make sure they get home," said the voice she was suddenly getting used to.

"I don't know." Ashlynn bit her lip, unsure whether to call her mom or just get out of there. "Heath, are you sure?"

"Of course. Like I said, I'm used to this. She usually listens to me when I say it's time to go. Even if she doesn't, I don't have a curfew anymore, so I can stay until she finally decides to leave or passes out. I'll even make sure Courtney gets home safely, too."

Everything in her was saying not to trust him. This was Heath

Lancaster. Star football player. College party boy. The guy who was the subject of most of her arguments with Victoria.

But what options were there? Her mom would kill her if she got home later, and she knew there was no way Victoria and Courtney would leave, not unless she physically dragged them—which was *not* going to happen.

"Okay, fine. I cannot believe I am trusting you, but I don't really have a choice, do I?"

"Not really, no." Heath grinned. There was the cocky football player she remembered.

But back at home, getting ready for bed, she couldn't shake the unsettled feeling. Could she really leave for Colorado knowing this was the type of thing Victoria would be doing every weekend? The thought pounded through her as Ashlynn searched through her drawer for her large clip, the only thing that could hold her long, thick, brown hair while she washed off the remainder of her makeup.

"It's not like me being here has made a difference the past few months, anyway," she muttered to herself, allowing the cold water to run down her face longer than normal.

Victoria was one of the main reasons Ashlynn had hesitated making the decision to go to Denver Christian. She knew it was where she was supposed to be, she could tell from the moment she'd set foot on the campus. But she also knew her lifelong friendship with Victoria was never going to be the same once she left. She was sure that was the main reason she'd got so angry at the party.

Ashlynn climbed into bed, too tired to think anymore. In the morning, she told herself, once Victoria had time to sleep off her inevitable hangover, Ashlynn would go over and assure her that while things would be different, they would still be best friends. Maybe that would help.

But morning seemed to come far too early.

"Ashlynn…. Ashlynn, honey. Wake up."

Ashlynn opened her eyes to see her mother sitting on the edge of her bed. She'd switched the lamp on, and Ashlynn couldn't read the expression on her mother's face. Outside her window, she could see it was still dark. *Something's wrong.*

"Mom? What time is it? What's going on?"

"Honey, let's go to the kitchen and get some tea so we can talk."

Ashlynn rubbed her eyes then saw the time—3:09. "You want to have tea at three in the morning? Mom what is going on?" She could hear the shake in her own voice.

"Ashlynn, I—I'm so sorry." Her mom took her hand and gave it a squeeze. "There was a car accident on the edge of town."

The edge of town. Somebody coming home from the party. *Victoria.* "Mom. What are you saying?"

Her mom was trembling now. "Honey, I just got off the phone with Victoria's mom. She—Victoria. She was in the car."

In an instant, Ashlynn was out of bed, rushing to find her sweat pants and tennis shoes.

"Ashlynn, what are you doing?"

"If Victoria was in the car, we need to get to the hospital." She fumbled with the pants, her hands shaking. "I need to see how she's doing."

Her mom turned away, as if unable to look her in the eyes. "Ash, she's not at the hospital." Her mom swallowed, blurted, "She was pronounced dead at the scene."

Dead. No. This was impossible.

The room began to blur. Ashlynn numbly felt her mom guide her back to her bed.

"No, Mom. It—it must be a mistake. I just saw her a few hours ago."

Her mom stroked her hair, gently helped her under the covers. "Victoria's mother said they think she died instantly. The driver was rushed to the hospital with some injuries, but nothing critical."

Ashlynn pulled the covers up to her neck, fighting the urge to hide. "Do Heath's parents know?" she finally asked.

"Heath?"

"You said the driver was taken to the hospital. Do Heath's parents know he's in the hospital?"

"Ashlynn, Heath wasn't driving. It was one of the girls on the cheerleading team. Courtney, I think?"

A flicker of rage coursed through her. *How could he have let her get in that car with Courtney?*

But her anger at Heath quickly turned to disappointment—in herself. How could she have trusted Heath Lancaster to do the right thing? She'd spent the last two years trying to convince her best friend he was a bad influence on her, yet Ashlynn herself had believed him when he said he'd make sure nothing happened to Victoria.

That thought sent the grief right back to the front of her emotions. The tears held at bay since her mother came into her room spilled hard and fast, and she could not stop them. Her mother held her while she cried, rubbing her back and telling her how sorry she was.

Ashlynn barely noticed. All she could think of was that she was never going to see her best friend again. That, and she would never make the mistake of trusting Heath Lancaster with anything.

Ever again.

August, present day

Ashlynn gripped the steering wheel and took a deep breath as the "Welcome To White Lake Sign" came into view. The bright sun of summer hit the sign like a spotlight, and several kind of wildflowers lined the field around it. It looked exactly the same as it had the last time she'd seen it, ten years ago.

She reached into her console and grabbed her phone, hitting the hands-free button on her dashboard. "Call my roommate," she said to the empty car.

"Calling Isabelle Parker," the phone's automated voice stated.

"Did you make it?" Isabelle, Ashlynn's roommate and best friend for the last decade, sang out cheerfully.

"I'm about to pull into town, but I'm turning around. Belle, I can't do this."

"Pull over."

"What? I wasn't serious about turning around."

"Just pull over. It's the middle of nowhere, right? You'll be fine."

Ashlynn rolled her eyes at the jab at her small town, but she pulled her CRV to the shoulder of the road. "Okay, I'm parked on the side of the road now," she huffed.

"Good. Now close your eyes."

"Seriously?"

"Just do it."

Ashlynn sighed, took her hands off the steering wheel, and closed her eyes. "Fine, they're closed." She knew what Isabelle was trying to do, she did this with her clients all the time, but it did mean she was not still a little annoyed that this tactic was now being used on her.

"Now take a deep breath, and let it out." Isabelle paused, obviously listening to hear if Ashlynn would do it. "Keep your eyes closed, and just listen. Father, I lift Ashlynn up to you. You know how heavy her heart is. Please help her process the painful memories this place holds for her. Be with her as she ministers to her parents during this tough time. I also pray your healing hand on her father, Paul. Lord, we know that you can and do heal, and we ask that you take this cancer away from him and that it be for your glory. Use this to draw him to you. Father, I also ask that you give Ashlynn people to stand beside her during this time. Remind her that we are here for her, and provide people in White Lake to be there for her, as well. I ask this all in Jesus' name. Amen."

Ashlynn wiped a stray tear from her cheek. "Thank you, Belle. I needed that more than I realized."

"That's why I'm here. Remember, I'm only a phone call away if you need me. And if things get too hard, I have several sick days saved up. I can find a sub for my classes and be there as quickly as my Prius will take me."

Ashlynn laughed at the image of Isabelle speeding across the interstate in her electric green Prius.

"See?" Isabelle laughed. "You sound better already."

"That's because the thought of your wind-up car getting you here quickly is comical."

"Whatever, I would probably only have to stop for gas once."

Ashlynn laughed some more, then put her hands back on the

steering wheel, shifted into gear. "Thanks, Belle. Will you stay on the phone while I drive into town?"

"Of course. Is the town the same as you remember?"

Ashlynn chuckled as she drove down the small main street with its two rows of brick buildings that served as downtown. "Yeah, it's pretty much the way I remember."

"Describe it to me. I keep picturing Stars Hollow from Gilmore Girls when you talk about your hometown."

"Definitely not that picturesque. The Dalton Diner sign has green letters now instead of blue, and they got a fresh coat of paint on the building."

"Oh, big news."

"The craft store changed its name, again. I think that place had twelve different names when I lived here. And the library looks exactly the same, including the sign out front announcing the retirement of the librarian."

"The sign has announced her retirement for ten years?"

"More like fifteen. I think I was in eighth grade when she retired. It started out as an announcement. Now it's more like a tribute."

"I seriously need to visit this place," Isabelle said genuinely. Having lived in the Denver metro area her entire life, her friend had always been fascinated with the quirks of small town life. "What are you passing now?"

Ashlynn glanced out the passenger's side window. Immediately, she felt her mood change. "The cemetery." Her voice sounded empty. Broken.

Isabelle's tone softened. "You can do this, Ashlynn. Remember, you aren't alone. How close are you to your parents' house?"

"I'm about to turn onto their street." Ashlynn could see the house already. "Hey, my dad got a new car. He didn't even tell me! I thought he'd never get rid of that stupid pickup truck from 1975." A flash of learning to drive in the rusted old yellow Ranger flickered through her mind.

"I'm glad you made it, Ash. Don't forget to take a picture of the house for me! You always talk about the view."

Ashlynn smiled at her best friend's attempts at distraction. "Okay, I'll hang up and take the picture now. Thanks again, Belle."

Ashlynn hung up as she pulled her CRV behind her mom's Civic in the long driveway. Shouldering her purse, she surveyed the view Isabelle had been talking about—the lake, White Lake, for which the town was named on one side, and the town square on the other. Home.

She snapped a picture on her phone, then snagged her backpack and headed up the driveway to the house, typing out a message to Isabelle with the picture as she walked.

She was so lost in her phone that she felt her foot hit something in her path. *What in the world....*

She jerked her head up—and knocked it straight into the shoulder of a man leaving her parents' house. Pain surged through her nose, and she yelped—then realized her nose was bleeding, a lot.

"Ashlynn? Is that you?" The man with the offending shoulder asked. "Are you all right?"

Squeezing her nostrils tight to keep the blood at bay, she looked up again, realizing with a start who the man was. "Heath Lancaster?" she asked in complete shock. "What are you doing at my parents' house?"

"Let's get you inside. I want to take a look at your nose and make sure it isn't broken." His voice was cold, almost clinical, and he started to lead her to the house.

Her mother came out the door at that moment. "What happened? Is she okay?"

"I'm fine, Mom. We just literally ran into each other as he was coming out of your house." Ashlynn said pointedly, not liking being talked about while she was standing right there. Why did Heath Lancaster know her mom so well?

"I want to make sure her nose isn't broken, but other than that I think she's fine," Heath said, ushering her up the steps.

Heath led her to the living room, where her father was sitting in his big armchair.

"Doc, what did you do to my girl?" her father asked, though Ashlynn could tell he was trying not to laugh. *Doc?*

"Your daughter here decided she needed to text and walk at the same time. She ran right into me." Heath sounded annoyed.

"And you didn't move out of the way?" Her father's gruff voice had a hint of joking in it.

"I tried, she was determined." Heath added, this time sounding more amused.

Ashlynn looked between the two men, confused. Her dad was not unfriendly, but it took quite a while before he got comfortable enough with someone to joke around with them. Something else was weird, too.

"Heath, did my dad just call you 'Doc'?" She cast him a puzzled glance.

"Well, yeah. Didn't your parents tell you I'm treating your dad's cancer?" Heath held up his doctor's bag like it was no big deal.

Ashlynn looked up at him in disbelief. Heath Lancaster, the star football player and party boy of White Lake High, was not only back in White Lake but he was a physician? What happened to the football career that was so important to him?

"Here, Ashlynn," Heath said, breaking her of her thoughts. "Let's take a look at your nose."

She nodded, then winced as he leaned down to move it in several different directions.

"The good news is it doesn't look broken," he said finally,

straightening up. "But it will hurt awhile. Put some ice on it, and take some ibuprofen if the pain is too much to handle."

He barely looked at her. *Probably remembering the last time we saw each other, wondering if I'm going to start screaming at him again like at Victoria's funeral.*

"Thanks," she said vaguely, still trying to process what exactly was going on.

"Paul, I'll be back by to check on you in a couple of days." Heath shook her dad's hand as he walked back out the front door, still not meeting her eyes.

Ashlynn watched him go, then turned to her mother. She opened her mouth, but her mother spoke first.

"Paul, why don't you go lay down, and I'll make sure Ashlynn gets some ice for her nose and gets all settled in." Ann headed to the kitchen, giving Ashlynn a look that conveyed they would talk after her dad left the room.

Her father nodded, then slowly stood and wrapped his daughter in a hug. "I'm glad you're home, Ash." His smile warmed her, and she felt a flash of guilt for having stayed away for so long.

Ashlynn smiled back, though she couldn't stop herself from thinking how weak his hug felt. It was strange seeing her father like this. Cancer.

A moment later, her mother returned with an ice pack, a bottle of water, and ibuprofen. "Here, take these and put this on your nose." They settled on the couch. "So in all the excitement, I didn't get a chance to tell you I'm so glad you're here. We have missed you so much, honey."

"Thanks, Mom. I'm sorry it has taken something like cancer to get me back here."

Her mom gave her a reassuring smile. "We understood. Now about Heath…."

"Yes, about Heath." Ashlynn shot her mom a look. "Why didn't you tell me he was Dad's doctor? I didn't even know Heath was back in White Lake."

"I know you and Heath have a, well, complicated past. So I decided I would just tell you in person. I didn't expect you to literally run into him before I had the chance."

"So tell me now. How did this happen? I always thought Heath would be playing professional football. When I didn't hear about that happening, I just assumed he ended up coaching at a Junior College or something."

Her mother took a deep breath. "You didn't hear? I thought everyone posted everything on social media these days." Her mom sounded truly surprised.

"No, I don't really use my social media that much." She hesitated admitting why and decided to just be honest. "And I purposefully don't follow anyone from White Lake other than you and Dad. I made my profile secret so no one can find me, either. After Victoria, well—it was all just too much at first. And honestly, it was kind of nice to just forget about what was going on here. I know that probably isn't very healthy, but they say therapists make the worst patients." Ashlynn shrugged.

Her mom just gave her an understanding smile. "I guess that makes sense. Anyway, after Victoria died I think it made Heath rethink his priorities. He dropped his football scholarship and quit the team to focus on getting into medical school, follow in his father's footsteps. He got into the University of Texas Medical School in Houston. He did his residency, and we all thought he would end up working at some major hospital in Houston, but then his father announced his plans to retire, and Heath moved here to help with the patient load. He plans to completely take over the practice within the year, I think."

Ashlynn blinked. "Frank is retiring? He's barely sixty. Is there a reason he's retiring so early?" Something was not adding up.

"I'm not sure. When he told your father and me, all Frank said was he was ready to spend more time with his family. I asked Heath about it, and he said essentially the same thing."

"So if Frank isn't completely retired yet, why didn't he continue seeing Dad? I can't imagine Dad liked the idea of a young guy, his own daughter's age, taking care of him."

Her mom chuckled. "You know your father well. He didn't like it at first. But apparently Heath did a lot of work on the oncology ward during his residency, so it just made sense. Since then, Heath and your dad have formed a very unlikely friendship. He's one of the few people your dad actually listens to."

Ashlynn sat there a few moments, trying to soak it all in. Heath Lancaster, the man who caused the rift in her friendship with Victoria before her death, the man who promised her he would make sure Victoria and Courtney would get home safely from that party, was back in White Lake. He was not playing or even coaching football, he became a doctor, and he was friends with her parents.

She rubbed her head. This was all too much.

"So this whole time on the phone when you were telling me Dad really liked 'Doc Lancaster' and was listening to him, you weren't talking about the Doc Lancaster who is close to his age who's been practicing for over thirty years, but rather about his not-quite thirty-year-old son?"

Her mom laughed. "See why I wanted you to see it in person? You wouldn't have believed me if I'd told you over the phone, would you?"

Ashlynn just nodded. Her mother was right. And besides, she had so much else going through her mind that this extra bit of information would have made it even harder to come home, especially since she had no idea how long she would be here.

Her mom stood. "Do you need help bringing your things in?

We've got a little while before dinner so I can help you get settled in. I've got your old room ready for you."

Ashlynn smiled, and led her mom to her car. They were able to get almost everything in one trip, and together they carried it to her childhood bedroom.

Opening the bedroom door, Ashlynn froze. It was like time had gone backwards, and suddenly she was eighteen again.

"I wasn't sure what you'd want to keep or get rid of, so I basically left it the way it was," her mother said, coming up behind her. " If it is too painful, let me know and I can take it all down."

Ashlynn slowly looked around. Her old boy band posters still hung on the walls, her cheerleading pompoms still rested on her dresser, and the little scraps of printed-out Scripture verses were still tacked on the walls in various places around the room.

She sucked in a deep breath when she got to the picture collage she'd put together shortly before graduation. It was filled with pictures from her childhood—several of her family, and a few from youth camp and mission trips she'd taken over the years with church.

The majority of the pictures, however, were of her and Victoria, spanning over their lifelong friendship. Near the middle was a picture from their junior prom. Ashlynn smiled at the group photo—Victoria and Heath next to Ashlynn and her date for the night, Kevin Dalton. She gave a small laugh, remembering how right after that picture she and Heath had gotten into an argument. Again.

She turned back to her mother. "It's fine, Mom. Really. I was so scared to come back here because of all the memories. But the truth is, I was suppressing the memories of the good things, too, and that's not healthy. I—I think I needed the reminder."

Tears threatened.

Her mom gave her a tight hug. "Spoken like the counselor you are," she said with a chuckle. "Now if you want to change out of that blood-stained shirt, Mrs. Fisher is bringing over dinner in about thirty minutes."

"'Mrs. Fisher From Church,' Mrs. Fisher?" Ashlynn asked, surprised. As the church secretary and youth volunteer, Mrs. Fisher was someone Ashlynn had known well in high school, but she didn't know her parents had grown close to her. A lot of things had changed since she'd left home.

"Yes, she and several of the other ladies in my Sunday school class have been taking turns bringing meals the last few weeks while your dad has been getting worse. They knew you were coming into town today, so they thought tonight would be a good night."

"Did you just say your Sunday school class? Since when do you go to Sunday school?" Ashlynn felt dizzy from all this new information.

Her mother smiled and headed for the door. "This was another conversation I was waiting to have until I saw you in person. Go ahead and change, then come into the kitchen. I'll fill you in before Mrs. Fisher gets here if there's time."

Ashlynn just stared at the closed door for a few moments, rubbing her throbbing temples. So much for not much changing about White Lake.

Chapter 2

Heath slammed his truck door shut and made his way up the cracked walkway to his front door. Literally running into Ashlynn and almost breaking her nose was not how he'd wanted their first interaction in ten years to turn out. If he had known she was coming today, he would have scheduled Paul's visit for that morning. Honestly, he was hoping he wouldn't have had to interact with her at all.

His front door creaked as he opened it, and he tossed his doctor bag on the chair in his living room, then headed to the kitchen to figure out dinner.

Based on her reaction, he could tell Ashlynn had no idea he was treating her father, or that he was even back in White Lake. He supposed that shouldn't have surprised him. Her parents were probably afraid their daughter would never come back if she knew she'd have to see him again. After all, she had told him at Victoria's funeral she hoped she never saw him again, and he had a feeling she still felt that way.

He opened the pantry door, saw nothing that appealed to him, and banged it shut. *She's just going to have to deal with me being around.*

He wasn't the one who'd left and decided not to come back for ten years. He moved to the refrigerator. Nothing there seemed appealing either. He was just about to call and order a pizza when his phone rang.

Some of his bad mood faded when he saw who was calling. "Hello, Mom."

He could hear her smile over the phone line. "Hello, Heath. Have you started making dinner yet?"

He stifled a chuckle. "No, I just got home."

"I'm glad to hear it. I made homemade ravioli, and there is way too much for just your father and me. Come join us? I haven't seen you in a couple of days."

Heath grinned. That was a much better option than pizza from a place that also served as the bait and tackle shop.

He decided to walk the few blocks to his parents' house. Maybe it would help him clear his head. By the time he got there, his mood was decidedly better.

"Heath! I'm so glad you came over." His mother hugged him like it had been months since she'd seen him and not days.

He laughed and followed her into the dining room, where his dad was already sitting at the table. Heath sat down to join him, then realized there were four place settings.

"Who is joining us for dinner?" he asked.

His mom waved a hand like it was nothing. "Oh, I just ran into Rachel Patterson at the grocery store. I was telling her about my homemade ravioli, and she said she always liked it when I brought it to the church potlucks, so I invited her over, too. Didn't I tell you that on the phone?"

Heath sighed. First the run-in—literally— with Ashlynn, and now matchmaking attempts by his mother. What was next? "No, you didn't. Probably because you knew if I thought this was a setup, I wouldn't come over."

"She's a very nice girl, Heath."

"I'm sure she is, Mom. But I just moved back. I really don't want to start a relationship right now."

"It doesn't have to be some big serious commitment, Heath. It's just dinner. Plus you need more friends."

"I have friends. You mean I need more female friends."

She opened her mouth to reply when the doorbell rang. She practically ran to the door. "Oh, that'll be Rachel."

"Did you know about this?" He asked his dad while the ladies chatted briefly in the entryway.

"Not this time. I learned my lesson after Erica," his dad said seriously.

His most recent girlfriend, Erica, had been the daughter of one his dad's friends in Houston. She was one of several daughters of his dad's doctor friends that he'd been set up with over the years. When things did not work out between them, Erica's father stopped inviting them places and generally gave his dad the cold shoulder.

He heard footsteps and turned to see his mother and Rachel walking into the dining room.

"Rachel, you remember my husband, Frank, and my son, Heath?"

Rachel, a pretty blonde with bright blue eyes, flashed a smile that was so big it almost seemed fake. "Yes, nice to see you both again. Heath, are you enjoying being back home in White Lake?" She said it like they were old friends, though in reality he had probably only spoken to her twice before.

"I am enjoying it. I appreciate it much more now than I did as a teenager," he said honestly.

"Really? I figured you missed high school. I mean I know you almost seemed a little angry, but you were a star football player, the teachers and students all loved you, you were dating a great girl—" She looked like she wanted to eat her words. "I'm so sorry. I—I almost forgot about what happened with Victoria."

Heath tried to smile. Was this day over yet? "It's okay, it was a long time ago. We all wanted out of this small town in high school, though, right? Now I see what it has to offer." He broke off a piece of bread, hoping someone would change the subject.

"So, Rachel, what do you do now?" His father asked and Heath gave him a silent thank-you for reading his mind.

"I work at the craft store. It's a lot of fun getting to talk to people in the town, people watch, that sort of thing." She sipped her iced tea, and then spent the rest of dinner talking about the latest gossip and news in town.

Dinner and dessert were finally over, and Rachel declared she had a fairly early morning so she was going to head on home.

Heath, wanting to be polite, walked her to the front door.

"Tell your mom thanks for inviting me," she said as she was leaving. "I had a great time." She gave him a big flirtatious smile, as if hoping he would ask her out just the two of them.

"I'll let her know. Thanks for coming," Heath said awkwardly. He was really bad at awkward situations.

Heath found his parents watching the news in the family room. "She's gone."

"So what did you think?" His mom sounded hopeful.

Heath sighed. "Mom, I appreciate the thought, but please just ask me next time before you set something up like this."

"You didn't like her." His mom said it as a statement, not a question.

"It wasn't that I didn't like her. She's just not my type. She still expects me to be popular, goofy, 'Football Star Heath' from high school. I'm not that guy anymore. I want to date someone who knows me and appreciates who I am now, not someone who wants what they think I was over ten years ago."

His dad chuckled. "I hate to break it to you, Son, but that may be hard to do in White Lake."

"I know. But I am choosing to have faith that God will provide someone for me to love and marry when the time is right."

"I am sorry, Heath. I just want you to be happy," his mother said genuinely. "After Jessica," she paused taking a deep breath, "well you're my only child now and I want what's best for you."

He sighed. He was sure his mom was putting all her hopes for both of her kids onto him now, whether she meant to or not. "I know that, Mom, and I love you for it. I am happy, though. A lot happier than I ever was in Houston."

"I'm glad. Now can you stay, or do you need to get going?"

"I should get going. I have things to do around the house before calling it a night." They stood for hugs. "Thanks for dinner it was great as always."

The cool air hit his face and he was glad he had chosen to walk over. After multiple trips down memory lane today, a brisk walk was exactly what he needed.

Ashlynn arrived at the lake early the next morning to find it just as she remembered: calm and quiet. She sat at her favorite bench and pulled out her Bible and notebook.

Last night, and the conversation with her mother, replayed in her mind as she sat and surveyed the smooth water, the lush grass, the tress surrounding the entire lake.

She closed her eyes, let the morning breeze wash over her. *Father, thank You for giving me the courage to finally come back here. Thank You for always being with us, even when we try to ignore what You're prompting us to do. Thank You for never giving up on us, for constantly pursuing us.*

What her mother had told her was the answer to a prayer she'd had since she was fifteen. After dinner, her mother had explained how when her father had been diagnosed with lung cancer, she'd decided she needed some support, so she'd gone one Sunday to the church Ashlynn had spent so much time at as a teenager. Her mom was immediately welcomed, and after several weeks, she realized how just much God loved her and that she could not go through this journey, or any of life, on her own. She had wanted to tell Ashlynn sooner but decided it was better explained in person.

Ashlynn was overjoyed. Since she'd accepted Jesus in high school, after a friend had dragged her along to youth group, she'd been praying that both her parents would come to know Jesus for themselves, too. Now that her mother had, she could just keep hoping and praying her father would too. She knew convincing the strong former factory worker that he needed anyone other than himself would be difficult, but with his possibly terminal illness, it was even more important.

She thought about how Isabelle had prayed Ashlynn would have other believers to stand by her. She never imagined that prayer would be answered in her mother. Opening her notebook, she started a poem. It was rough, but it expressed how she felt. Most of her poetry was that way, just a way to express what she could not say out loud, not intended for anyone but her, and her Savior.

When she finished, she set her pencil down and looked away from the lake, toward the trees. Birds chirped their morning songs in the background, and it was just windy enough to make the branches sway slightly. In Denver, she loved having the Rocky Mountains practically in her backyard, but there was nothing like the lake in White Lake.

Footsteps sounded in the distance, and she turned to see someone running along the path around the lake. As the runner came closer, she realized she recognized him.

Heath.

Taking a deep breath, she gave a polite wave and nod as he approached.

"Ashlynn?" he panted, stopping to stretch against the back of the bench, his muscles stretching out his shirt, making it obvious working out was a regular occurrence for him.

"Heath," she said, keeping her voice even.

"I, uh, see you've discovered the best place in White Lake, too?" He sounded as uncomfortable as she felt.

"I used to come here every morning before school. I did grow up here, you know." She couldn't keep the barb out of her tone. *Why was he still standing there?*

"Right, uh, look." He stopped stretching, and he looked at her seriously. "I know we have a complicated past, and I'm probably the last person you wanted to see at your house. Or this morning. To be honest, I wasn't real thrilled when I heard you were coming back to town, either. I think my ears are still ringing from the verbal lashing you hurled at me at Victoria's funeral."

The nerve.... She opened her mouth to speak, but he continued.

"That being said, your dad has become more than just a patient to me. He's become a friend, and for his sake, I think we should call a truce."

A truce? She stared at him blankly. Was that even possible?

He wiped a bead of sweat off his brow with the back of his hand and stared back at her. If this was anyone other than the man responsible for her best friend's death, she probably would have found it cute, that the combination of discomfort and unwillingness to back down. Instead, she was just annoyed.

"A truce?" she finally said aloud.

"Look, I'm not asking you to like me. I'm not asking you to forgive me. I'm not asking you to pretend the events of ten years ago didn't happen. I'm not even asking you to be nice to me when we're not around your parents. All I'm asking is that you tolerate me and we attempt to get along while we are around your parents. The rest of the time you can avoid me all together if you want."

Ashlynn sighed. He was right. "Okay. Fine." She stood to shake his hand. "We'll call a truce."

Shivers ran down her spine as their hands made contact, and she pulled her hand away quickly.

Then, giving him a faint smile, she picked up her things and walked away without saying anything else.

Heath put his headphones back in his ears as he watched Ashlynn walk off and restarted his run. As he picked up speed, he thought about their conversation.

He'd realized last night on his walk home that if they were going to both be in Ann and Paul's lives, they needed some sort of truce. So why didn't he feel better about it?

Because you wanted more. You want her to forgive you, to accept the person you are now.

That was silly, he knew. She was never going to forgive him completely. He didn't blame her—he didn't fully forgive himself. So why did he want it so badly?

When he'd first moved back to White Lake, he'd expected a lot of hostility about what had happened to Victoria, only to discover no one really blamed him for the accident. Enough people had been there that night to see her and Courtney drinking, and they knew she took risks. Sure, he still had people like Rachel who still figured he was the goofy football player from high school, but most people seemed to accept he was not the same cocky, angry kid he had been back then. A part of him was hoping Ashlynn would feel the same.

Somewhere behind the anger and annoyance he'd felt yesterday, when she first ran into him—literally, lay a desire for them to be able to start over. If the stories her parents told him were true, she had become a fairly successful counselor at a prominent Christian counseling center in Denver and was very involved in her church there. If they didn't have such a negative history, she was definitely someone he'd be interested in having as a friend. *Truth be told, she's the type of woman you'd be attracted to, Lancaster.* At least, in any other circumstance.

Out of breath, he slowed to a walk, and then stopped. Bending at the waist to stretch, he paused to listen to the birds singing to each other. Something about this lake made everything seem better.

With his eyes still closed, he turned his thoughts above. God, am I crazy to want Ashlynn to see me as more than just the dumb kid who drove a wedge between her and her best friend? Give me guidance in how I'm supposed to interact with her during the time she's in town. Help me to be content with the situation the way it is.

He paused, starting the walk back to his house. And as he walked, he murmured another prayer. "Father, please also be with Paul. Draw him to you in a way that he can't help but see who you really are."

Chapter 3

Ashlynn walked into the church building Sunday morning, overcome with a wave of emotions. She knew it would be hard, coming to the place where her best friend's funeral had been held, but she also felt a sense of coming home. She'd spent a lot of time at church during high school, between youth group and local missions, and it had become like a second home to her.

"How are you doing?" Her mother asked as they walked into the sanctuary.

Ashlynn smiled at her. "I'm doing alright. I'm a little on emotional overload right now—memories of Victoria's funeral flooded with memories of all the great times I spent here in high school, but mostly I am glad to be back and finally be sharing this with you."

Her mother smiled back as they sat down next to Heath's parents, Frank and Lori Lancaster, and exchanged hellos. It was good to see her mother had found a church community to support her. She couldn't believe her mom had never mentioned it. Why had she kept it a secret?

The worship pastor started the first song, and as they were singing, Ashlynn heard someone come up their row.

"May I join you all?" the deep voice asked.

Ashlynn looked up, shocked to see Heath standing there. *Heath went to church?* Back in high school, he had laughed at her for suggesting they all go to youth events together.

She moved over so he could sit between her mother and his. As the service continued, Ashlynn tried not to be distracted by Heath sitting there. It was good he was at church, right? She'd been hearing whispers about how much he'd changed in the last ten years. Could part of his change be that he'd actually become a believer? She shook her head, trying to push thoughts of Heath out of her mind and instead focus on the sermon.

After worship, they gathered in the back of the sanctuary.

"We really are so glad you're back. This place has missed you!" One of Ashlynn's old youth leaders, Pam, hugged her tight. "Now tell us all about Colorado. How's your job?"

Ashlynn smiled, glad to catch up with her and some of the other ladies from church. "My job is going really well. I work for a large Christian counseling group, and I get to counsel young people who have been through trauma or suffered a great loss." People like her, Ashlynn thought. Seeking counseling after Victoria's death had been the best thing she could have done—and it ended up leading her to what she soon learned was God's plan for her life: helping others in this way, too.

"Oh, my, I bet that is hard at times!" Pam looked impressed. "So what about the rest of your life? Anyone special?"

Ashlynn tried not to groan out loud as Pam winked. It was the same question she got all the time from people at her church in Denver. She knew they meant well, but it was annoying. What was she supposed to say? "Well, I've had exactly two relationships in the last five years, and one ended because he was intimidated by my career, and the other ended before it started for no apparent reason?"

No, that was not what Pam, or anyone else who asked this question wanted to hear.

Suddenly, she heard Heath coming up behind her. "Sorry to interrupt ladies, but I promised Ashlynn's mother I would get her home soon."

Pam nodded. "Well, it really was good to see you Ashlynn." She waved cheerfully. "We'll catch up some more soon."

"Thank you for the escape," Ashlynn whispered as she and Heath walked toward the front of the building. "They were starting to ask personal questions, and I wasn't sure how to answer."

"No problem. I could tell things were getting awkward. Plus, I really did tell your mother I would make sure you got home."

"Where did she go? Is everything all right?" *Is Dad okay?* she wanted to ask, but didn't dare.

"I'm sure it is. Your dad just called and wanted her to come home. He does that most weeks—doesn't like your mom spending too much time with 'church folk.'" Heath grinned. "I think he's just lonely."

Ashlynn smiled back. "That does sound like my dad. I think he would get more mad if I was late coming home from a church thing than he would if I came home late from anything else."

"I can't imagine you coming home late, ever." Heath chuckled.

She found herself laughing with him. "You're right. I was too afraid of getting in trouble or breaking any rules."

They walked silently toward Heath's truck. He opened her door and she climbed in.

She took a deep breath when they were both buckled up. "Look, Heath, I'm sorry if I've been distant or rude. What you said the other day at the lake made a lot of sense. We should try to at least tolerate each other. Who knows? Maybe we'll even be able to get to know each other as who we are now, instead of who we were ten years ago."

"Are you saying you want to try to be friends?" Shock was evident both in his tone and on his face.

She thought a moment. "How about we start with friendly? I honestly don't know if we can ever truly be friends, but I am willing to try to be friendly."

"I think friendly sounds like a good idea."

They were still quiet, but the mood was lighter as they drove.

But as they pulled into her parent's driveway, Heath parked quickly.

"Wait, is that your mom?" He sounded concerned.

Ashlynn looked up to see her mother sprinting toward the truck.

"Heath, it's Paul! He just started seizing. I was picking up the phone to call you when you pulled in." Her mom's eyes were wide, and her face looked bone white.

Heath jumped out of the car and followed her inside the house, asking questions all the way: How long he had been seizing? Any other weird symptoms or behaviors?

Ashlynn had never seen her mother look so scared. Heath disappeared down the hall to the bedroom to check on Paul.

Ashlynn took her mom's cold hand, led her gently to the kitchen. "Mom, why don't I make us some tea while we wait to see what Heath has to say?"

As Ashlynn started the teakettle, she suddenly found herself thankful Heath was there, and able to help her father so quickly. For the first time, she realized, she was thinking of him as her father's doctor, not Victoria's old boyfriend. Maybe this "friendly" thing could work.

When the tea was ready, she set a mug in front of her mother.

"Mom why don't we pray while we wait?"

Her mother nodded, so Ashlynn grabbed her hands and they both bowed their heads.

"Father," Ashlynn prayed, "we come to You today, and we ask for healing. We ask that the seizures would stop and that You would reveal what is causing them. We pray for peace for Dad when he wakes up that he will not be too scared and will feel Your comfort." She paused trying not to choke up and cry. "Lord, we also pray for wisdom and guidance for Heath as he assesses the situation. Show him your constant presence and direction for what to do next. We pray this all in your son Jesus' name."

"Amen." A deep voice said from behind her.

She turned to see Heath leaning against the doorframe, his head also bowed in prayer.

Heath walked to the table and put a hand on her mother's shoulder, looked her directly in the eyes. His expression was kind, but serious. "I was able to get the seizures to stop for now, but I think it would be best for us to get him to the hospital in Pine Grove."

"It's spreading isn't it?" her mom whispered.

Heath tightened his jaw. "I am concerned this means the cancer could be spreading into his brain, yes," he said in a matter-of-fact, yet gentle way. "They have more equipment for me to monitor him there in Pine Grove, as well as constant trained nurses to assist if something happens quickly in the middle of the night."

"Do we need to call an ambulance?" Ashlynn asked.

"I called and the only one they have is in use, so it will be faster for us to take him." Heath looked at Ashlynn's mom. "Are you okay to drive, Ann?"

"I think so. I'll start gathering up his things and loading them in the car," her mom said, her voice surprisingly steady.

Ashlynn watched in shock as her mother headed back to the bedroom. She had been home less than a week, and already some of her worst fears were coming true. She turned to Heath. "I guess I should gather some things up, too."

She walked to her room in a daze, grabbed some items from her large suitcase, and threw them into her old cheerleading duffel, which she'd found crammed under her bed. Taking a deep breath she headed into her parents' room to see if her mother needed help.

She grabbed the oxygen tank from her mother's outstretched hand and followed her to their car, neither mother nor daughter saying a word.

When everything was packed in the back of the car, Ashlynn turned to see if her mother needed help with her dad, when she saw Heath already carefully guiding him to the car. Ashlynn almost fell over when she saw how weak and fragile her father looked. The man leaning almost entirely on his doctor for support looked close to death, and it was almost all she could do to not throw up.

She tried to compose herself and started rummaging through her purse for her car keys. She finally found them and walked shakily to her car as Heath settled her parents in the Civic, hoping she would be able to make the drive in one piece.

Heath made sure Ann really was okay to drive, then turned to head to his own truck so he could meet them there. That's when he saw Ashlynn walking toward her car, looking like she was about to fall over.

"Ashlynn!"

She turned, still looking completely out of it. *She's in shock.*

He jogged over to her. "What are you doing?"

"There isn't enough room in my parents' car, so I'm driving mine." She sounded like she was in a different world.

"No, you aren't. You look like you're in shock, and there is no way I'm letting you drive in that condition." He snagged her duffle bag so she didn't have a chance to protest. "I'll drive you."

She nodded slowly and followed him to his truck. He helped her in, then closed the door before placing her things in the back cab. He pulled out of the driveway and made sure Ann and Paul were right behind him.

"If you look in the glove box, there should be a bottle of water in there," he said in his "doctor" voice, then waited while she found it. "Drink that. It'll help calm your nerves."

She took a drink and then turned to him. "Thanks. I do feel better. I'm sorry I freaked out there but he just looked so close to death. I've never seen him like that." Her voice was a whisper.

Heath sighed. He still did not know this adult version of Ashlynn very well, but from what he sensed, she would want the truth, no matter how harsh it was.

"I'm not going to sugarcoat it. Your dad could be close to death. If the cancer has spread to his brain, then it will be a lot more aggressive and is usually a lot less responsive to treatment. I'm afraid it might be a matter of how long he has at this point."

He tried to sound pragmatic yet compassionate. Still, he knew it was a tough thing to hear.

"I knew I would probably have to come to grips with that reality, but now that it's here I—I don't know how to handle it."

"You handle it by leaning on those who care about you, and on God. It's the only way to get through something like this." He saw the look on her face and knew what she was thinking. Then he added gently, "Just like you did before."

"I was just hoping this would be different than before." She said it so quietly he was not even sure she realized she'd said it out loud. He felt for her, he really did. Even when his father had the heart attack and Heath had been faced with the possibility of losing him, at least Heath knew he would see him again. Death would not really be the end for his dad.

But for Paul, unless he finally decided to follow Jesus, it would be the end. He knew what Ashlynn was thinking: She was not sure she could handle another person she cared about dying without knowing Jesus. To be honest, Heath wasn't sure he could, either.

They spent the rest of the car ride to Pine Grove in silence. Once they pulled up to the hospital, Heath looked over at Ashlynn. "I'm going to need to help your dad inside and check him in. I called ahead so they are expecting us. Are you all right to go in with your mom and fill out any paperwork they need?"

She nodded, looking like she was switching gears to "action mode."

He got out of his truck and went over to Ann and Paul's car, helping Paul into the wheelchair that an orderly had brought out. He wheeled him inside the emergency room and went to the front desk.

"I'm Dr. Heath Lancaster from White Lake. I called requesting a room?"

In small towns it was fairly normal for neighboring towns to all use the same hospital. It was something Heath was still getting used to, but typically things still went faster here than in the large hospitals in Houston.

A young nurse approached. "Dr. Lancaster? I'm Wendy, the nurse assigned to you. Follow me and we'll get you situated. Is there family here to fill out paperwork?"

Heath nodded and pointed Ann and Ashlynn over to the reception desk before following Wendy to a small room.

He leaned down to his friend. "Paul, I'm going to have Wendy here check your vitals, and then we're going to send you down for an MRI, okay?"

"Whatever you say, Doc," Paul said wearily.

Heath tried to smile at him. This was going to be a long afternoon.

Ashlynn found a spot in the waiting room that was fairly secluded, yet close enough to the nurses' station to get information if they needed it. They had already filled out all the paperwork and had been there about an hour, and Ashlynn was getting restless.

"Mom?" she asked tentatively. Her mother had not said much since they arrived, but now she looked up at her daughter. "I think I'm going to walk around a bit, maybe go get some coffee. Do you want anything?"

"Thanks, but I'm all right. I think I'm going to try to read some," her mother replied as she pulled out a devotional Ashlynn recognized.

Ashlynn found a coffee cart, then decided to walk around the small hospital. She thought about her mom and how she was leaning on God and her church community now. She hated that it was her dad having cancer that finally led her mom to the truth of God, but still, she was so pleased that her mom had finally found it. She realized she should probably call the church office and let them know what had happened.

Now if only her dad would come to know Him, too. She did not know if she could handle another person she loved die without knowing Jesus. It was still something she struggled with every day with Victoria's death over ten years ago.

She walked past a small chapel and was about to go in when her phone rang.

"Hello? Mom? Okay, I'll be right there."

She headed back to the waiting room. Heath had some news.

Twenty minutes later, they were gathered in her father's room, waiting for Heath or someone to give them some answers.

"Hey, Dad. how are you feeling?" she asked her dad, who looked a little more alert.

"Annoyed. Doc told me he had news, and I'm sick of waiting," he said gruffly.

Ashlynn held back a laugh. Her dad hadn't changed much.

"I heard that, and I'm right here," Heath said, coming in the door and shutting it behind him. Ashlynn noticed he had a white lab coat on now. It was the first time she'd seen him looking like a doctor.

It was weird. Dressed like that, in this hospital room, she could almost forget he was the former high school football star and good looking "bad boy" that her best friend fell for.

Well, almost forget.

He motioned for them to sit. "I'm afraid these seizures do indicate what we had feared could happen." His voice was almost hollow, like he was reading a script. "The cancer has progressed to Stage Four and has spread throughout your body, including into your brain."

Ashlynn gasped, and her mother grabbed her hand. Paul just listened, his expression unreadable.

"So what does this mean?" her mom asked.

"There are some options. We can do another round of chemotherapy, followed by some new treatments that are still in clinical trials. But you do need to know there is a very good chance these treatments may not work. Your cancer is advancing very quickly, and so far it has not been very responsive to treatment. You also would not be able to do these treatments as outpatient like you were in the past. You would need to stay here in the hospital."

"I'm sick of treatments that don't work, Doc," Paul said in a matter-of-fact tone. "What are my other options?"

"Hospice care," Heath said with almost no emotion in his voice. It was as if he was speaking, but he was not really there.

"Hospice? Doesn't that mean it's over? He's ... dying?" Ashlynn asked quietly.

"Hospice will allow you to be comfortable. I will no longer be your treating physician, and you'll be in the care of nurses who will help you be as pain-free as possible in your final days. I can recommend some good groups that will come into your home in White

mend some good groups that will come into your home in White Lake and treat you, or you can check into a hospice house. Some people prefer their final days be at home, while others prefer to be away from home."

"Can we have a few moments to discuss all our options?" her mom asked.

"Of course. I'll leave you all alone to do just that. Page me if you have any questions." Heath walked out the door, closing it behind him again.

Ashlynn could not believe this was all happening, and so quickly. She needed some time to take it all in.

"Mom, Dad. I'll let you all discuss this in private. I'm going to go take a walk, maybe go visit the chapel. Call me if you need me."

With that, she hurried out the door.

Heath walked out of Paul's room, feeling like he was about to be sick. He had dealt with this kind of thing several times as a resident but this was different. He knew these people. They were his friends. Paul's soul was still in jeopardy. He tried to distance himself from the situation, tried to see it as any other patient, but he couldn't do it. Instead he just felt distant, like he was listening to someone else's words come out of his mouth.

He walked down the hospital hallway and found the chapel. As he quietly opened the door, he felt himself relax a fraction. This was exactly where he needed to be right now.

But when he walked in, he heard someone crying. He looked over and saw a young woman, kneeling at the front, head bowed down, her dark hair falling over her shoulders. Ashlynn.

He walked over to her, not wanting to interrupt, but also wanting to make sure she was all right.

"Father, please—please don't take him from me before he comes to know You. Please draw him to You." She was choking out the words in between sobs.

"God, I echo Ashlynn's prayers," Heath blurted, kneeling next to her. "Please bring understanding to Paul. Show him that You love him and want to welcome him home to You when his time here is over." He could feel his own tears begin to build.

Ashlynn looked up at him. "Heath. I didn't hear you come in."

"I came to pray for your dad. I saw you in here crying and wanted to make sure you were okay."

She looked up at him like she wanted to say something, but then broke down in loud, big sobs instead.

His heart broke for her. He knew she had to be thinking the same thing as him. Not again.

Without thinking, he pulled her into a hug and let her cry on his shoulder. It felt natural, and he gently patted her back.

"I won't tell you it's going to be okay," he said as she sobbed, "because I don't know that it is. But God will be with you no matter what. So will your mother, and the church community here. We've all got your family in our prayers, and we will all support you no matter what happens."

She pulled back a little. "We?" she asked, sounding surprised.

He tried to smile. "I count myself part of that community, yes. I know that may be hard for you to believe, but like I said, I've changed a lot since high school."

She looked like she was going to say something, but they were interrupted by her phone ringing.

"It's my mom. I'd better answer this."

He tried not to eavesdrop on their conversation as she sat next to him, phone cradled to her ear.

Ashlynn hung up, then slowly turned to him. "She said they've decided to go with a home hospice group."

"I'll walk you back to his room. I can make some calls and get him all set up, then get him released from here," Heath helped her stand, and they started back.

He had a feeling this would be the path they decided to take. He just hoped he and Ashlynn's prayers would be answered in time.

Chapter 4

Three days later, Ashlynn stepped inside the diner, smiling as the bell over the door rang. She was glad some things never changed.

It felt good to be out of the house. Since coming back from the hospital, she and her mother had stayed home to get the new hospice nurses acclimated to their house, as well as try to keep her father as happy as possible. They did not want to lose nurses because he was being his typical cranky self.

Heath had called her mother earlier to say he was going to stop by and check on Paul and see how he was doing. Even though he was not treating him any longer, he had promised them he would still stop by, though as a friend now instead of a doctor. Ashlynn decided this was the perfect chance to get out of the house. Not only would her mother have plenty of help with Heath around, but it would give her a good excuse not to have to see him. She was not sure she wanted to face Heath after the incident in the hospital chapel.

She still could not believe she'd broken down like that in front of him! Not just in front of him, on him. She could still smell his woodsy cologne if she thought about it. No, she needed to stop thinking about that. Just because he was the first man to comfort her or be there for her in a long time did not mean anything. This was Heath Lancaster, after all—her best friend's former boyfriend. Even without their complicated history, he was off-limits.

Ashlynn found a table in the diner and looked around while she waited for someone to help her. It had obviously been remodeled in the last ten years, but all the old charm was still there.

"Ashlynn, is that you?" She heard a familiar voice behind her.

"Whitney?" She was shocked to see her friend from high school and youth group standing in an apron, holding an order pad. "I didn't realize you worked here."

"I manage the place, actually. My husband's family owns it, and his parents decided to retire, so I took over the management responsibilities."

"Husband? You married one of the Dalton brothers? Carter or Kevin?" Ashlynn asked, truly surprised.

Whitney smiled. "Kevin. Carter is still doing the famous rockstar thing in L.A." She grabbed a coffee pot and mug and put it in front of Ashlynn. "What do you want to eat? I'll put the order in and make sure everything is running smoothly, then I'll come join you so we can catch up.

Ashlynn nodded and ordered the steak and cheese omelet. She sat drinking her coffee, thinking about how even though White Lake seemed the same, a lot had changed, too.

Whitney came by a few moments later. "Sorry about that, we just finished our big rush so my staff should be able to handle things without me for now."

"I still can't believe you manage this diner," Ashlynn asked as her friend slid into the booth. "Honestly, I can't believe you're still in White Lake. What happened to culinary school in Europe? You wanted out of this small town more than I did."

Whitney shrugged. "I went. I lived in Paris for two years and worked under some of the greatest chefs in the world." She paused and took a sip of her own coffee. "But I missed it here. Paris is great, but it's extremely lonely. And to make a very long story short, I fell for this guy, one of my coworkers. Turns out I wasn't the only chef he had eyes for, and the heartache was too much to handle. I decided to move back home for a little while and see what White Lake might have to offer. Kevin had just taken over the diner from his parents and needed someone to cook, so I took the job, and we started hanging out more and...." She giggled. "Well, now we've been married two years and I went from chef to diner manager."

Ashlynn smiled. Whitney and Kevin had both been friends of hers in high school. They never acted like there was anything more than friendship between them, but honestly she was not surprised they fell in love as adults. She was a little surprised that Whitney had come back to White Lake, but lately nothing was happening like she thought it would when they were in high school.

"So what about you? How are things in Colorado?" Whitney asked.

"Things are going pretty well there. I ended up getting my degree in psychology and then getting a master's degree in marriage and family therapy. I work in grief and trauma counseling now, mostly with kids and teens."

"Wow, that's great. I can totally see you as a counselor. You were always the one who knew when to just listen and when to give advice." Whitney took another sip and looked like she was thinking really hard about what she wanted to say next. "Look, Ash, I know it must be really hard for you to be back here. Not only because of the circumstances, but I also know the memories must be really tough. I remember praying for Victoria when we were in small group together at youth group. How much it hurt you that your friendship was suffering, and how much you wanted her to come to know Jesus like you did."

Ashlynn took a bite of her omlete "Wow, Whitney, this is really good."

Whitney smiled. "Thanks." She took a deep breath. "I know we lost touch, and part of that was my fault for not knowing what to say, or whether you even wanted to talk to anyone. But please know that I have been praying for you ever since that accident. And your dad is in my prayers now, too."

"Thank you, Whitney. That really does mean a lot." And she truly meant that. She forgot how well she and Whitney got along and realized she missed having her as a friend.

"Oh, and we have a group that meets every Wednesday morning here at the diner for prayer and support. It's early, around 5 a.m. since we open at 6:30, but I would love for you to join us tomorrow. We can pray for your dad together."

"I'll think about that," Ashlynn said honestly. She missed the community she had back in Colorado, and this may be a great way to reconnect with believers in White Lake.

Ashlynn walked into the diner early the next morning, right at 5 a.m. The closed sign was still on the door, but a sign under it said to come on in for the prayer meeting.

The bell tinkled as she opened the door, and she saw a few people already sitting down at a large table drinking coffee. She made her way over and saw Mrs. Fisher and Pam, as well as a couple of other ladies she recognized from church.

"Ashlynn, I am so glad you came to join us," Mrs. Fisher said warmly, standing up to give her a big hug, her small frame not stopping her from nearly crushing Ashlynn from the force of it.

"I'm glad to be here. And I'll be even more excited once I get some of that in my system." Ashlynn pointed to the coffee, and they all laughed.

The older woman waved over at Whitney, who was standing behind the counter. She came over, followed by her husband, Kevin.

"Good to see you, Ashlynn," Kevin said while Whitney poured the coffee.

Ashlynn smiled at him. "Good to see you, too. I hear you and Whitney got married! Congratulations. That's really great," she said sincerely.

Kevin had always been one of her better guy friends, the one she could always come to if she needed a guy's opinion or help with something. They were also often each other's dates to school and church events, but the two had always been simply good friends. She was glad that he had found someone who made him happy.

"Oh, and have you met Pastor Dustin?" Whitney said turning to the young gentleman approaching the table.

"I haven't. I wanted to after hearing you preach Sunday but didn't get a chance. It's nice to meet you, Dustin. I'm Ashlynn."

"Nice to meet you, too, Ashlynn. I've heard a lot about you. Your mother could not stop talking about how excited she was to see you come home," Dustin said, grinning.

Ashlynn just smiled. She was surprised the church had chosen someone so young to replace Pastor Todd, who had retired last year, but she was glad because he seemed to be a great fit for the church.

"Where's Charlotte this morning?" Whitney asked as she poured Dustin a cup of coffee as he sat down.

"My mother came into town yesterday, so she's staying at the house with her. Good thing, too. That girl is not a morning person! Takes after her mother that way," Dustin said, then, seeing the confused look on Ashlynn's face, added, "Charlotte is my five-year-old daughter. Her mother died a couple of years ago, so usually she's here with me on Wednesday mornings."

He said it kindly, then turned around and started talking to the other people at the table.

After a few minutes of everyone getting coffee and catching up with each other, Kevin stood up and cleared his throat.

"It looks like this might be everyone who is going to come this morning, so I guess we'll go ahead and get started." As soon as the words left Kevin's mouth, the bell above the door jingled, signaling someone else had joined them.

"Hey, everyone, sorry I'm late." The voice was deep, and familiar. Ashlynn turned around to confirm the identity of the latecomer.

Heath.

Heath should have realized someone would think to invite Ashlynn to the Wednesday prayer meeting. He had not seen her since they'd all left the hospital on Sunday. She was gone when he'd stopped by the house yesterday, and he suspected it was on purpose. Looking back, he may have over stepped his bounds in the hospital chapel. He was trying to comfort a friend, but as they'd already established, they were not really friends. Too much had happened between them. Now it just felt strange.

"Who wants to go ahead and get us started with prayer requests?" Kevin asked the group, bringing Heath out of his thoughts.

"I'd like us to continue to pray for Paul, Ashlynn's dad," Heath spoke up, looking at Ashlynn. "As most of you know, he was put on hospice this week, which means his time is more than likely coming to an end."

Ashlynn glanced over at him, a surprised look on her face.

"We will definitely continue to pray that he comes to know Jesus, as well as for the family during this difficult time," Mrs. Fisher said, nodding. "Is there anything else we can be praying for your family, Ashlynn?"

"I guess the only other thing would be that we can all come to terms with everything," Ashlynn said hesitantly, taking a deep breath. "I confess I've been struggling with it."

Heath saw Whitney squeeze her hand, and Ashlynn smile back at her in gratitude.

They continued taking a few other prayer requests, then spent the next half hour lifting them up. Heath might not like early mornings, he thought as he looked around the table, but he cherished these early Wednesday prayer meetings.

They dismissed right around six so Whitney and Kevin could get the diner open. Thinking he might skip his morning run to instead have breakfast with the group that usually stuck around, Heath spotted Ashlynn talking to Dustin, the pastor at White Lake Community Church.

A twinge of something, he didn't know what, twisted in his stomach, and he realized he did not like seeing the two of them being so friendly. Shaking his head, he decided he would go for that run after all.

Heath reached the lake and ran harder than he did most mornings, his thoughts on Ashlynn and Dustin talking at the diner. Why did it bother him so much? Dustin was a nice guy, and as a widowed, single father, he suspected it was only a matter of time before the ladies at church decided to set him up with one of the single women around town. Ashlynn made as much sense as anyone. So why did the thought of them together make him want to hit something?

He kept running, even harder now. He couldn't be jealous. Ashlynn could not stand him. He wasn't especially fond of her, either. She was still as pretentious as she'd been in high school. Though he had to admit she'd been on his mind a lot, especially since their encounter in the hospital chapel. Something about seeing the girl who had always seemed so strong and formidable suddenly being vulnerable and hurting tugged at his heart.

So maybe he did feel attracted to her. Who cares? It was not like it mattered—this was Ashlynn. Victoria's best friend. The person who blamed him for what happened even more than he blamed himself.

She was much better off with someone like Dustin, he told himself. And he needed to remember that.

After a typical morning seeing people with minor ailments, Heath took a quick lunch break and checked his phone for any messages or missed calls. He had mixed emotions when he saw his cousin Norah had called. Norah was an only child, and she and Heath's sister Jessica were the same age and practically best friends. Heath kind of saw it as his duty to protect her—the way he had not been able to protect Jessica. However, a call from Norah usually meant trouble, or at least drama. Norah was currently in the middle of a divorce after finding out her ex-husband, Tom, had been abusing their five-year old daughter, Madelyn. The last few months had been really tough on all of them, and Heath never knew if her phone calls were just because she needed someone to talk to, or if she'd found out some new information regarding Tom or the divorce.

He looked at his schedule and decided he had enough time before his next patient to give her a call. He hoped it wasn't anything bad.

"Heath! Thank you so much for calling me back." Norah's voice was a mix of frustration and relief.

"No problem, Norah. What's going on?"

"I have some good news, but I need a favor." She paused. "Madelyn and I are moving to White Lake!"

"Oh, Norah that's so great." They had discussed this possibility in the past, and he was glad she was going for it. "This will be a great fresh start for both of you."

"I know. Madelyn's and my therapist suggested a change of scenery, and I always loved visiting you all there. It seemed like the best place."

"I completely agree. So do you need help finding a place to live, or need a job?"

"I actually have most of the details worked out. My dad called your dad, and they helped me find a rental house, and Mrs. Fisher recommended me for the church secretary job." He could hear her take a deep breath. "The only thing is counseling. Our therapist obviously can't continue with us once we move, and she doesn't know any psychologists near the area. Do you have any contacts you could put me in touch with? I know White Lake doesn't really have any Christian counselors, but maybe in Pine Grove or another neighboring town?"

"I don't know of any right away, but I'll makes some calls and see what I can find out for you."

"Oh, thank you so much!" Norah was practically gushing, which made him smile. Heath was glad to hear a little hope in her voice again.

Heath hung up, thinking about Norah and Madelyn's situation. He had a few friends in counseling, but they were all in Houston. The only person he knew in White Lake with any counseling experience was Ashlynn, but she probably wasn't going to be in town very long. He wondered if she might have any contacts here that she could call.

And with that, he picked up his phone again.

Chapter 5

Ashlynn's dad had just fallen asleep when her phone rang. Seeing it was Heath, who she only added to her contacts because he was her father's doctor- nothing more, she answered it hesitantly. "Hello?"

"Ashlynn? This is Heath. I have a favor to ask."

After he'd explained the situation, she told him she would make some calls and to meet her at the lake after his last patient so they could talk more about the situation in person.

She got off the phone with her last contact and headed to the lake. Heath was already there, waiting for her at the bench.

"Ashlynn, thank you so much for doing this. Did you find out anything?" He stood to greet her.

"I called four places within an hour's drive. Three have absolutely no openings. The fourth was going to check with the part-time counselor to see if she'd be willing to take on another patient. But I'm going to be honest—they didn't sound very hopeful about that."

"I was afraid of that." He sat back down. "What am I going to tell Norah?"

She sat down next to him for a few minutes, trying to come up with a solution. "Let's go for a walk," she said suddenly.

"What?" He looked completely confused.

"I think better if I'm moving around. Plus, the lake always seems motivating, inspiring even. Maybe I'll get an idea while we're walking. And you can tell me more about the situation so I can see if I can come up with an idea."

He nodded and stood, offering his hand to help her up, as well. She took it hesitantly, and then dropped it when she stood up. They walked the lake in silence for a couple of minutes.

"So tell me a little more about this situation," she asked, going into work mode. "Why is it so important that Norah and Madelyn move here?"

"Their current counselor thinks a change of scenery would be good for her. Norah agrees, and her lawyer thinks it would be a good idea, too; it proves she's trying to do what's best for her daughter after finding out everything that happened with her ex-husband."

"Okay. So why White Lake? Surely there are other places she could go that would provide a change of scenery but have better access to care."

"I know she wants to be around family. Her parents are both in Houston and cannot both leave their jobs to move with her, and our families have always been close, so I think it made sense to her. Their counselor also thinks a smaller town with a slower pace might be good for Madelyn. Fewer strangers and tense situations."

"That's a good assessment. I don't know Madelyn, but a lot of times for kids in these situations, that is true." She paused. "So why is this so important to you? I know she's your cousin, but you seem to have a very personal stake in all this."

He stopped walking a minute. "I guess because after what happened with Jessica, she's the closest thing I have to a sister."

"Jessica?"

"I'm not talking about this." Distance crept into his voice.

"Not so fast." She crossed her arms. "You call me, out of the blue, ask me to help you with your cousin who needs the advice of a counselor, tell me you are close even though I've never even heard of her, then say it's because of something that happened to someone else I've never heard of, and expect me to just drop it? I did not go to school for six years to let you hold this kind of thing in."

He sighed like a man resigned. "Jessica was my sister."

He started walking again, fast. She raced to catch up.

"You had a sister?" She softened her tone.

"Yes." He didn't look at her. "She was about sixteen months younger than me, and a month older than Norah. The three of us were extremely close growing up."

"What happened?" she asked quietly.

"When she was ten, she hadn't been feeling well for about a week, but we all just thought she had some kind of bug. When she fainted at school, my dad decided to take her to his office and do some bloodwork. It came back saying... she had leukemia."

He stopped walking again.

Ashlynn stopped, too, and put her hand on his shoulder, encouraging him to continue.

"She started treatments at MD Anderson, and even though they made her really sick and she lost her hair, she was a fighter. She went into remission a little while, but then it came back, and this time it didn't respond as well to the chemotherapy and radiation. So they decided to do a bone marrow transplant. Siblings are usually the best match, so I was tested to see if I was or not."

He paused for a moment.

"So... were you a match?" Ashlynn asked.

"I was. So they did the procedure, and she went into remission again. We were all so excited, and she was thrilled that she got to spend her thirteenth birthday at home instead of in the hospital. Becoming a teenager was a huge deal to her, especially since she wasn't sure if she would make it that long. We threw her a huge party, and she went back to school and joined the band. We thought she was finally going to have a normal life. But six months later, the cancer came back again, even more aggressive than the second time." He cleared his throat, and she wondered if he was close to crying. "They tried a lot of different treatments this time, but nothing worked. She died. Two weeks before her fourteenth birthday."

They stood there a moment, silent. Everything she wanted to say fluttered through her mind, then fizzled out.

Finally, she kept it simple. "Heath, I'm so sorry. I'm sure that was hard on your whole family."

"It was."

They started walking again, but much slower. Ashlynn noticed the trees starting to show just a hint of yellow though she knew it would be much longer before the leaves really started to change colors. "So you were fifteen then?" she asked. "That was about a year before you moved here."

He nodded. "My parents had a really hard time being in Houston after she died. Everything reminded them of the daughter they'd lost. I think my dad felt like he should have been able to save her. I mean, he was a doctor, yet his own daughter died from cancer."

"Survivor's guilt is hard to deal with." She squeezed his shoulder.

"My dad and Dr. Graham, who was practicing here at the time, were good friends. When Dr. Graham decided to retire, he called my dad to see if he wanted to take over the practice. My parents decided it was the best thing for our family. So we moved here."

"Is that part of why you were so angry when you got to White Lake?" She raised an eyebrow.

"You caught on to that, huh?" He chuckled.

"I could tell even then that you seemed to have a chip on your shoulder. Now looking back, I can see you were hurting."

Now he full-out laughed. "You could say that. I was the opposite of my parents. While it was too hard on them to be in the same house my sister was in, to go to school functions she should have been a part of, for me it was really comforting. It made me feel like a part of her was still around. When we left, I felt like we were leaving her memory behind. It felt like running away to me."

"Everyone grieves differently."

"I can see that now. At the time, though, I was just angry."

Ashlynn was quiet for a few minutes. "So after Jessica died, Norah became like your sister?"

"Like I said, we were all really close growing up. Her family lived just a few blocks away, and we did things together all the time. Norah was at the hospital visiting almost as much as I was. She even volunteered to get tested to see if she was a bone marrow match if I wasn't. After she died, the two of us clung to each other. I think the only person more upset than me about us moving to White Lake was Norah. She came and visited every summer, though."

"I think I vaguely remember Victoria saying something about a cousin of yours that she met. Did she know about Jessica?" Ashlynn asked suddenly.

"She was one of two people in White Lake I ever told about Jessica, yes."

"Who was the other one?"

"Kevin Dalton. After we all went to prom together, he and I kind of became friends. He kept trying to get me to come to church, but didn't pressure me about it. One day I just kind of spilled my guts about why I was so angry with God and didn't want to go to church."

"What changed that?" she asked.

He started to respond when her phone started ringing.

She looked at the phone. "It's the counseling center in Pine Grove."

They grinned, and she felt her hopes begin to rise.

But minutes later, those hopes had fallen. Ashlynn hung up the phone, discouraged. After everything Heath just told her, she really wanted to give him good news.

"The part-time counselor called back, and she doesn't have any time in her schedule to add another patient." She gave him a sympathetic look. "I'm so sorry."

Another bench was just ahead, and Heath sat down heavily.

"What am I going to do?" he asked.

Ashlynn sat next to him and put a hand on his shoulder. *Good question.* "Have you considered using a non-Christian counselor? There are plenty out there who counsel from a Christian point of view and would be willing to take that into account. There are even several who are Christians but may not have an exclusively Christian practice."

"I suggested that previously, but Norah had a really bad experience with a non-Christian counselor right after this all came out. They claimed to be but their methods definitely went against a lot of what she believes in. She said she would never go that route again."

"That makes sense." Though she still did not know what the solution was.

He looked up at her, an almost desperate look on his face. "What if you helped them? You know, just temporarily until we could find someone else?"

Ashlynn pulled back "Me? I don't even live here. It wouldn't be a long-term solution."

"I know, but hear me out. They could get moved here and get settled, Norah could start her new job, Madelyn can enroll in kindergarten for the fall, they can get established and maybe make some friends. Then maybe they'll feel comfortable enough that a longer drive to someplace like Houston, if that's the only option, won't feel like such a big deal."

Ashlynn twirled a piece of her hair, thinking about the idea. She had some clients in her practice in Denver who drove from smaller towns because of the reputation of the center. She had one client who drove four hours, first once a week and now a couple of times a month because finding a reputable, Christian counselor was important to their family. Maybe she could help Madelyn and Norah get settled, then help them find a good place somewhere within driving distance. She was unsure how long she would be here, but she had her clients covered for the next three months so it would be at least awhile. It would give her something to do other than just sit and worry about her dad too.

She looked back up at Heath "Okay. I'll do it. Call Norah and see if that is an option that might interest her."

Heath jumped up, obviously excited. "Thank you, Ashlynn. You have no idea how much this means to me."

She smiled at his reaction.

"You're welcome! Now, do you have the pastor's number? I want to see if there's a room we can use at the church." As she talked, she mentally reviewed a checklist of all she needed to do to prepare for a new patient.

"No need. The space next to the clinic used to be a counseling center. My dad owns that part of the building, too, and we haven't even changed the setup. I even have the cleaners go over there and make sure it's still in good shape. You can use it as your office if you want."

Ashlynn was surprised. "Why do you still have it set up for a counseling center? Wouldn't it be nice to expand the clinic?"

"Honestly, I've been praying about it, but I keep feeling like God is telling me to keep it like it is. I would love to find someone to re-open the counseling center. White Lake could use one."

Ashlynn thought about that for a moment. How often did her clinic have more counselors than they really needed? They always tried to make sure everyone had a full enough schedule to not only be making enough money but also make it worth their time. It kind of seemed selfish to have a clinic that had that many trained therapists when there were areas that had a definite shortage, or none at all.

"Ashlynn?" Heath said.

"Sorry, I tuned out for a minute."

"I was just saying we should probably head back. I need to call Norah and see what her thoughts are. I was planning on stopping by your house later this evening to chat with your dad. If it's okay, I can let you know then what Norah says."

"That sounds great. And give her my number. Let her know she can call me if she has any questions or wants my office number in Denver to check references or anything."

When Ashlynn got home, she thought about what she had learned this afternoon about Heath. She had no idea he had a sister. His attitude when he first came to White Lake made so much more sense now. He'd been angry, and grieving. Poor guy had lost not only his sister, but also his entire life up until that point.

She remembered Victoria telling her at the time to go easy on Heath, that Ashlynn didn't really know him, that he was different than he appeared and had been through a lot for someone his age. Victoria was one of the only people who'd really known Heath, the real Heath, back then. He had kept such a big part of his life a secret—probably because it was easier than talking about it. Seeing this vulnerable side painted a completely different image of him: the side that cared so much for his sister that he'd go through a painful medical procedure. The side that reached out to Ashlynn, even, despite their complicated past and even more complicated present. The side that did what he could to help out his cousin.

She could see what made someone like Victoria fall for a guy like that.

And if she was not careful, Ashlynn herself could fall for a guy like that. Which was exactly why she had to be careful.

Chapter 6

Heath walked up to the Wilson's front door slowly, still more than a little uncomfortable about sharing all of that private information with Ashlynn that afternoon. On the one hand it felt nice to have it more out in the open. On the other, well—he was being vulnerable with Ashlynn Wilson. The fact that they'd even been able to talk without screaming at each other over the last few weeks was nothing short of a miracle.

Ann answered his knock. "Heath, good to see you! Paul's awake and was just asking if you were coming by soon."

"Thanks, Ann." He smiled, stepping into the house. "Is Ashlynn here? I have something I need to talk to her about before I go back and see Paul."

"I'm right here," Ashlynn said, coming into the living room and motioning for him to sit on one of the couches. "Have a seat. Did you talk to Norah?"

"I did. She said if I trust you, she trusts you, and it sounds like the perfect temporary solution."

"Great!" Ashlynn looked happy. "Tell her to have their current counselor email or fax over their records so I can review them before we get started. Can I use the fax machine at your office?"

"I actually have an extra line we can set up in the counseling facility. That way if you have any other communications needs, it'll be all set up. Now, she did ask about payment. Her insurance covers most of it, but she wasn't sure since you weren't with a group practice how that would work."

"Tell her not to worry about it. I'd have to go through my clinic in Denver, and get approval to see her while I'm on family medical leave, and it's just way too much of a hassle. I'll just see them at no charge."

He blinked. That was completely unexpected. "Are you sure? That's very generous of you."

"I'm sure. The last thing Norah needs to worry about right now is a bunch of paperwork and delays. I want to help her and Madelyn."

"Thanks, that really means a lot. To me and to them."

Ashlynn just smiled. "Just let me know when I can get into the building to set up everything and start going over their records. Now let's you get back to see Dad. He's been getting cranky wondering what was taking you so long," she said laughing.

Heath headed to Paul's room. Paul Wilson liked to talk a tough game, but the man's bark was much worse than his bite. He knew it was strange the two of them had formed such a friendship, but he was grateful for it. The man was funny and proved to be a great conversation partner, even when they didn't always see eye to eye.

"It's about time you showed up." Paul's gruff voice greeted him as Heath pulled up a chair to the side of the bed.

"Nice to see you, too. How are you doing?"

"Oh, you know, other than the whole dying thing, I'm doing pretty well." Paul made a face.

"Well, it's good to see you haven't lost your sense of humor yet," Heath joked.

"Actually, I'm doing pretty well. The nurses are taking good care of me, and I feel better than I have in a long time. I may even be able to get out of the house a little while tomorrow. They said I seem stable, and I'm not getting any worse, though I'm not getting any better, either."

"That happens a lot of times once cancer starts to spread. It hits hard really fast, but then it settles for a little while. I think maybe God uses it to let people do things before they go."

"Now what did I tell you about bringing God into our conversations?" Paul said irritably.

"That you get enough of that from your wife and daughter. And what did I tell you in response?"

Paul chuckled. "That if I really cared that much I would have kicked you out a long time ago."

Heath laughed, too. "And you haven't, so I'm going to keep bringing it up. It's not too late for you. God still loves you, and he wants to welcome you home when you die."

"If that's true, why did he give me cancer in the first place? It doesn't seem very loving."

For the first time, Heath noticed, Paul actually sounded curious, not just skeptical.

"I can't answer that," Heath said. "But there have been some good things that have come from this."

"Like what?"

"Your wife came to accept Jesus, which has opened her up to a lot of great people who will take care of her when you're gone."

"Okay, that's true. What else you got?"

"Ashlynn finally came home. Haven't you been saying for months how much you missed her being here?"

"That's true, too. You guys don't seem to hate each other as much anymore, either."

"You're right," Heath said. "We've come to understand each other a lot more. See? It's not so hard to see how God can use these experiences for good."

"So what if you are right? What if God does love me and He uses this whole thing to bring about good things. Why would He want someone like me? All I've done my entire life is mock people who use religion as their getaway. I even mocked my own daughter."

"Paul, God wants all of us, sins and all. Do you remember me when I was in high school? I was a wreck. All I cared about was football and parties. I made one bad decision after another. It took making a decision that cost someone her life before I woke up and realized how stupid I was being, and that I needed Jesus in my life. If He can love me after all that, He can love anyone."

Paul thought about that for a while. "I'll think about what you said. And I'll keep reading those books of Matthew and John, like you asked me to."

"You've been reading them?" Heath asked, surprised.

"Yeah. I wanted to find something that proved it was all a bunch of nonsense."

Heath laughed. "How's that working out for you?"

Paul just gave him a dirty look. "Hey, Doc?"

"Yeah?"

"Just for the record, no matter what my daughter and whoever else in this town think, I don't blame you for what happened with that accident with Victoria." Paul looked thoughtful, and his gruff tone had turned sincere, something Heath had only heard from him a couple of other times. "It doesn't matter that you left her there— she still got into a car with someone who had been drinking. And I may not know much about this forgiveness thing you keep telling me about, but if God is real and does love us, I'm pretty sure he'd want you to forgive yourself for that one silly mistake."

"Thanks, Paul." *Easy for you to say, but it's not that simple.*

"Now get out of my room, I want to take a nap," Paul said, switching back to his grumpy exterior.

Heath stepped out to let him get some sleep. *God, I hope this conversation had an impact. Please continue to reveal yourself to Paul.*

Ashlynn leaned against the counter in the kitchen at Whitney and Kevin's two-story farmhouse, watching her friend cook dinner. Whatever she was making smelled delicious.

"Thanks for inviting me over for dinner, Whitney." Ashlynn grinned.

"No problem," Whitney said, shaking spices into the pan, her hair tied back in a loose ponytail. "We both wanted to catch up with you, and what good is it being a chef if I can't spoil my friends by cooking for them?"

"Whitney's right! We've both missed you," Kevin said, gathering forks and knives from the drawer. "Tell us how things are going."

"Pretty well. There isn't much change in my dad. He's has a little more energy, so he's been able to leave the house some, but the seizures are still fairly regular." Ashlynn shrugged. "We know it's only a matter of time."

"Have you had any opportunities to talk about Jesus with him?" Whitney asked gently.

"No, he changes the subject any time my mom or I bring it up. But Heath actually has. He said during their conversation the other day that it was the first time Dad ever sounded like maybe he was interested in knowing more. Apparently he's also been reading Matthew and John out of a Bible Heath gave him."

"That's really good, Ash!"

"I know. I'm just trying not to get my hopes up."

"Speaking of Heath," Kevin said as he started setting the table, "it sounds like the two of you have been getting along a lot better. I heard you're even going to start counseling his cousin and her daughter?"

"Yes, at least until we can find a more permanent solution." Ashlynn remembered the way Heath had talked about Norah, how protective he'd seemed. A thought struck. "He told me the two of you are pretty good friends. Can I ask you something?"

"Sure, but I can't guarantee I'll be able to answer it."

"What exactly happened with him after Victoria died? My mom said he dropped his football scholarship and decided to go to medical school, but is there more to it than that? He really does seem like a completely different person and I just…." She couldn't figure out how to say what she was feeling.

"You're unsure if someone can really change that much, is that it?" Kevin said.

"I guess so."

"Look, I can't go into everything that happened after Victoria died, because that's Heath's story to tell. I can tell you that it completely changed him. I was skeptical at first, too, but this version of Heath is more who he really is. I didn't know him before he moved here, but from what his parents have said, this is more like who he was before they moved here."

"Before Jessica died," Ashlynn said thoughtfully.

"He told you about that?" Kevin sounded shocked.

"Wait, who's Jessica?" Whitney asked from the table.

"Oh, I'm sorry, I assumed she knew." Ashlynn said feeling badly.

"His sister," Kevin answered Whitney, then turned back to Ashlynn. "It's fine. But, if he told you about that, then you know how messed up he was when he got here. It also means he really trusts you."

Ashlynn thought about that. She knew not only from her years as a counselor, but also from her own experience, that grief changed a person. People often became the worst version of themselves while they were grieving. Knowing that Heath was grieving, or refusing to grieve, the death of his sister while they were in high school did bring a new perspective to things.

The fact that he trusted her was a big deal, too. He'd seemed to dislike her about as much as she'd disliked him. For him to change his mind was significant.

"Can I ask another question about Heath? A more personal one?" she said after they had all sat down at the table and blessed their meal.

"Again, you can ask," Kevin said. "I'm just not sure I can answer."

Ashlynn thought about how to phrase her question without making it sound like she had a crush on him, which she most certainly did not. "Why isn't Heath married? Surely a good-looking doctor and former college football player had no problems finding a date."

Whitney almost choked on her water.

"Why do you ask?" Kevin looked amused. "Are you interested?"

"No, I'm just curious!" Ashlynn's cheeks flushed pink. "Trying to put together more pieces to the puzzle."

If she were honest, if there was no history between them, she would be interested in Heath Lancaster. He was an attractive guy who obviously cared about his patients and his family and friends. He seemed loyal, too.

"If you say so." Kevin gave her a pointedly skeptical look. "It's really Heath's story to tell, but I will say the girls he has dated haven't worked out, mainly because they couldn't really understand why work and church his top priorities.

Sounds like he hasn't met the right kind of girl.

After dessert, Kevin headed to meet a couple of guys to play basketball. Ashlynn helped Whitney clear the table, then they curled up on the couch with coffee.

Whitney gave her a sly look. "So now that Kevin's gone, tell me why you're really so curious about Heath."

"Really—I'm just trying to put together who he really is. He's over all the time to see my dad, and I'm going to be working right next door when I start counseling his cousin and her daughter. I feel like I should know more about someone I spend so much time with."

"Are you sure that's all? Look, I know we haven't kept in touch, and a lot changes in ten years, but there's a lot of you who's still the Ashlynn I knew growing up. You like him, don't you?"

Ashlynn took a breath. "If I'm honest, I could. But I can't. Whitney, he was Victoria's boyfriend. And we do have a history. Even if we're both different people now, those things still happened. We can't just pretend like they didn't."

"True. But you *have* both changed. And you can't punish him, or yourself, over events that happened a decade ago. If you like him, go for it. Don't use the excuse that he's a part of your past to keep yourself from being vulnerable—and possibly finding love."

They were quiet a moment as Whitney's words sunk in.

"I… I'm just not sure that's possible," Ashlynn said. "I don't even know if we can truly be friends after, well, everything."

"Then start there. Hang out with him, get coffee, go on walks, and just get to know each other. Don't let the past stand in the way of what could be a great friendship. And who knows, maybe even more."

Dressed in athletic shorts and a T-shirt, Heath approached the basketball court, happy to see his friends. He didn't get together with them often enough, but when they did, it always made him want to do it more often.

"Heath, glad you could join us!" Kevin called out, as some of the other guys from church gave nods and waves.

Heath noticed Dustin, the young pastor, had joined them, too. It was the first time he'd seen him outside of church or their prayer meetings without his young daughter, Charlotte.

"Glad to be here. Dustin, good to see you here too," Heath said.

"Thanks. My mom's thoroughly enjoying being Grandma right now." Dustin laughed. "She practically begged me to go do something so she can spoil her granddaughter."

"I bet it's nice having her around to help out., Kevin said, tossing the ball in a practice shot. Some of the other guys gathered on the other side of the court, doing their own warm-ups.

"It is." Dustin snagged the ball, dribbled, then attempted his own shot. "It was hard to move away from her and my father, especially after Emily died. But I knew this was where God wanted us. The church here has been a great fit. For both of us."

"And I'm sure the ladies at the church have all tried to find you someone to help with Charlotte, too, right?" Kevin chuckled knowingly.

"Oh, yeah. The matchmaking in this place is unreal. I think they've tried to tell me about every single lady in the church."

"Hey, at least they don't have your mom trying to do the same." Heath chimed in, remembering the Rachel episode a few weeks ago. Since this, his mom had laid off, but he knew it was only a matter of time.

"Speaking of being set up, I had an interesting conversation with someone tonight at dinner asking me why you weren't married yet, Heath," Kevin said.

"Really?" Heath asked. "Who was that?"

"Ashlynn." Kevin smirked.

Heath shook his head. "Well, there you go—it wasn't anyone

who is actually interested, then." Still, he had to admit he was curious as to why she'd asked about him.

"Oh, I wouldn't be so sure about that. She got very defensive and was a bright shade of red when I asked why she cared."

"She seems like a great girl," Dustin said. "Why wouldn't she be interested?"

Heath looked at Kevin. "He doesn't know the story, does he?"

Kevin just shook his head.

Heath nodded Dustin's way. "Ashlynn and I have a long and complicated history. Her best friend, Victoria, was my girlfriend back in high school and my first year in college. Ashlynn and I didn't exactly get along. We both fought for Victoria's time, and I usually won. I think it drove a wedge in their lifelong friendship."

"Victoria?" Dustin looked like he was thinking. "Wasn't she that young girl who died in the car accident?"

Heath nodded.

Kevin clapped him on the shoulder. "Well, just so you know, Ashlynn was asking a lot of questions about your life. She seemed to understand that who you were in high school isn't who you are now. Or who you really were then. She told me you told her some other secrets, too." Kevin gave him a significant look.

Heath knew what he meant and nodded. *Jessica.*

"That's a big deal, and she knows it," Kevin said, bouncing the ball, then making a final practice shot. The ball swirled around the net and swooshed through. "So don't count her out, okay? There may be hope for you two, even after everything that's happened."

Heath tried to take it all in as the game started in earnest. Maybe Kevin was right. Maybe he and Ashlynn needed to try again as friends. He'd think about it later. Right now, it was time to play some basketball.

Chapter 7

Ashlynn could not remember the last time she'd felt this nervous about anything. She was just meeting Heath at the diner for coffee—it wasn't such a big deal.

But if it wasn't a big deal, why did you change your outfit three times? She tried to quiet the voice in the back of her head as the little bell over the door to the diner tinkled, and she looked around for Heath. She spotted him at a booth in the back of the diner.

He already had a coffee there for her. She slid into the booth opposite him, trying to calm her nerves. *Relax, Ash.*

"Hey, thanks for coming!" His eyes crinkled with a big smile, and he had a dimple in his left cheek. Why had she never noticed that before?

"Thanks for inviting me. So you said you wanted to talk?" she asked, taking a sip of her coffee.

"I realized that we've been spending a lot more time together, but we still don't really know each other. Then I ended up telling you a huge part of my life, and when you didn't run screaming, I figured we might actually have a shot at being more than just 'friendly' and actually being friends."

Ashlynn smiled. "Of course I didn't run away. I appreciate you feeling like you could trust me enough to share that part of your past with me. It did shed some insight into who you are, and why you were the way you were in high school."

"Exactly." He grinned mischievously. "So I figure it's your turn. Tell me something I don't know about you. If you're willing to give this a shot that is."

"Okay, I'm in. What's something you want to know?"

"What made you decide to go into counseling?" He said it as if he already had the question ready.

She paused, trying to decide where to start. She might as well be as honest and open with him as he had been with her. What did she have to lose?

"Well, as you probably know, when Victoria died, I decided to go to Colorado early. I wasn't able to stay in my dorm room yet, but the girl I was supposed to room with said I could stay with her family till school started. So that's what I did. But when I got there, I found out they were actually her foster parents." Memories swirled as she talked. That girl was Isabelle, and that summer had turned out to be a life-changer in more ways than one.

"Oh, wow," Heath said, looking genuinely interested and not just polite.

"Turned out it was the longest foster home she'd ever been in, and they treated her like a real daughter. They treated me like one, too. That summer was really good for me—to just be away from everything that had happened here. My parents are great, but back then my mom wasn't a Christian, and neither she nor my dad understood why I was so devastated. See, the worst part about losing Victoria wasn't just losing her. It was my fears. I knew Victoria wasn't a believer. Trust me—we'd had that conversation many times."

Heath was quiet, and she paused to gather her thoughts.

"And Heath, I'll be honest." She took a breath. "I blamed you a lot for the rift in Victoria's and my friendship, but honestly you were only part of the problem. A lot of the problem came from the fact that she didn't understand why I felt like I could share things with Whitney and my other youth group friends that I couldn't share with her. So I'm sorry for making you feel responsible. It wasn't fair to you." It was true, she realized. She'd put a lot of unfair blame on him.

"Thank you," Heath finally said. She could tell her words touched him from the way he was looking at her. "To be fair, I did fuel some of the conflict, though. It was part of me trying to get Victoria 'on my side,' which was just mean of me." He nodded his head, then, toward the other people in the diner, who Ashlynn just now realized were all watching them. "Why don't we take these to go and head for a walk? I think this conversation may be better away from the White Lake gossip train."

Ashlynn nodded and let him go up front to pay and get their drinks to go. They headed to the lake.

"Anyway," Ashlynn continued as they began their walk, "that summer was good for me. Isabelle, my roommate, and her foster parents, Joan and Chris, were believers and really great. They could tell I was struggling, so Isabelle suggested I try counseling. Being in the foster system, she'd been going to therapy most of her life, and it was actually one of her counselors who'd led her to Jesus, and to Joan and Chris. So I decided to go. It helped so much. Getting to talk about what had happened, and having her point out things to me that I didn't realize I was feeling, was really helpful. I continued throughout college."

"So is that what made you decide to make a career out of it? Your positive experiences?"

"In part. I struggled with what I wanted to major in and finally picked psychology, mostly because I found it really interesting. I was also helping in a youth group, and one of the young girls came to me for advice—a lot. I realized I really enjoyed helping her. So I talked with my counselor, and she told me she thought it would be something I'd be good at. I ended up getting my master's in marriage and family counseling with an emphasis in child psychology. I loved all the internships and getting to learn about how the brain works. My counselor worked with me a lot, and when I graduated, she helped me get me a job at her clinic."

"That's really great, Ashlynn," Heath smiled at her. "It sounds like you took your own experiences, and now you use them to help others."

She blushed. "So what about you? What made you give up the football dream and become a physician?"

"Honestly, being a doctor was always the real dream."

"Really?" Ashlynn was surprised.

"Really. When Jessica was in the hospital, I was fascinated by what the doctors were doing. It was the first time I'd ever really paid attention to what happened in a doctor's office, and I loved the idea of helping sick kids. I talked with my dad and some of his colleagues, and I got to shadow the pediatric oncologists at MD Anderson while Jessica was there. Truthfully, I only played football in Houston because that's what you do in Texas, and I was good. And when we moved here, football was the only thing I still had from that life."

That made sense. Still, she hadn't realized.

He cut his eyes at her. "As you know, by that point I was really angry, especially with my parents, so the last thing I wanted to do was follow in my dad's footsteps and become a doctor. I decided to pursue football. I never thought I'd actually get a scholarship anywhere, especially not a major school like Texas, so when I did, I went with it."

"Then why did you go back to the original dream?" Ashlynn was sure it had to do with Victoria, but she wanted to understand what had made the change.

Heath sighed. "When Victoria died, I realized how stupid I was being. Her death made me evaluate my life, and I realized I hated the person I had become. I didn't like being the angry kid, and I didn't really want to be a football star. I wanted to be a doctor. So I dropped the scholarship, quit the team, and joined the pre-med program. I thought I'd be behind since I joined a year late, but I liked all the classes and was good at them, and I was able to take summer classes, so I was actually accepted to medical school early."

"Nice!" She was impressed. "So what made you decide to come here and be a family practice doctor instead of going into oncology?"

"My dad needed me." He said it simply but with finality, like that was all he wanted to say on the topic. "Hey, look at that!" He pointed as two ducks chased each other.

She decided not to push it. This had been a really good start.

Two weeks later, they were sitting by the lake again, this time having a picnic and learning more about each other. This time it was the lighter-hearted topic of hobbies. Except for Heath, his mind had just been blown.

"But you were a cheerleader!" Heath said, surprised.

Ashlynn had just told him one of her favorite things to do was watch sports, and she might have well just told him she planned to go swim with sharks.

"Cheerleaders can't like the sports they cheer for?" she asked, eyebrows raised and a tone of indignation in her voice. He had to admit, she looked adorable.

Heath just laughed. "Most of the cheerleaders I know haven't the slightest clue about the sports they are cheering for. Victoria hated it when I even brought up football." He was glad Ashlynn no longer winced every time Victoria's name was mentioned.

"Well, then, that is something we had in common, isn't it?" She popped a potato chip in her mouth. "You want to know the truth? I only became a cheerleader because Victoria begged me to try out with her. Once I made the team, I realized White Lake's women's sports weren't that great, anyway, and the best way to stay close to all the action was from the sidelines. Even if that meant wearing a skirt and shaking pompoms around."

"So what's your favorite sport to watch?" he asked.

"Baseball," she said, not missing a beat.

"Really? You know you're from Texas right? You're supposed to say football." He gave her a look of mock hurt.

She shrugged. "Baseball is just so fascinating! It's such a mental sport, but you also have to be super athletic. You have to be good individually, but it's also about the team. Plus, anything can happen. You can be down by five runs and still win the game in the ninth inning. Look at the Royals last year!"

She said it with more passion than he'd seen from her since... well, come to think of it, since she'd yelled at him after Victoria's funeral.

He laughed. "Hey, you don't have to explain it to me. Did you know I played baseball back in Houston, too?"

"Let me guess. Shortstop?"

"How did you know that?"

"Easy. You were a running back, so you're fast and athletic. Everyone knows your most athletic guys play shortstop."

"Okay, I get it, you know your stuff. So do you have a favorite team?"

"I really started loving the sport in college, so I follow the Rockies." She grinned. "Though I must say, watching the 'loveable loser' Cubs do so well this season has been super fun. Okay, your turn. What's something you like to do in your spare time? Other than sports."

He smiled, thinking about his latest project. "I bought this old house, right on the edge of town, just about a mile from this lake actually." He glanced in the direction of the two-story farm-style house, picturing the old wood, the big wraparound porch, the barn in the back yard. "I love working on it. Building things for it, fixing things, updating things—it's been a lot of fun. I've actually thought it would be fun to buy old houses like that and flip them, make them a home for someone."

"Can I see it sometime?" she asked, sounding like she meant it.

"Of course!" The thought made him oddly happy. He glanced at his watch. "We better get heading back. Norah and Madelyn are expecting us at the clinic."

"I'm glad they're eager to keep going after our first session. The first one can be a little hard." She helped him gather up their things, and they headed to the truck.

When they were driving, she turned to him. "So, Heath, I have a question for you, but it has to stay between us. Is that okay?"

"Sure," he said curiously. They were getting along a lot better, but he was shocked she would trust him with a secret.

"When you said you were hoping someone would reopen the counseling center next to your office, what exactly did you have in mind?"

He was not expecting that kind of question. "Honestly, I don't really know. I know I'd want it to be a Christian counseling center. As a Christian, my faith is important to me, and Norah has told me a lot about Christian counseling versus some of the other kinds she's tried. Other than that, I'm not sure. I guess I was hoping someone would be interested, and then I would pray about it and see if I thought they would be a good fit for the town, and then rent the space out. Why do you ask?"

She took a deep breath. "What if I told you I was thinking of asking if I could rent out that space?"

Heath could not believe what he was hearing. "*You* want to open a counseling center in White Lake?" He honestly could not think of a better person to run something like this in White Lake. Did that mean she'd be staying there for good? Could *Ashlynn* really be the answer to his prayers?

"I've been really enjoying working with Madelyn. She is such a sweet girl, and I can tell she benefits from being in a smaller town. It got me thinking about how there's not really a place for people who live in smaller towns around this area, but the counseling center I work at in Denver is overrun with counselors. It doesn't seem right!" She looked a little shy now. "And honestly, I forgot how much I love White Lake. It really feels like home again. I realized I was running away before, and now that I'm back, I'm kind of sorry I ever left."

"What about your friends in Denver? Your roommate Isabelle? And your church community there?" By now he knew how important her friends were to her. This would be a big change for her, but he couldn't deny he hoped she'd do it.

"I've been talking with Isabelle. She hates the idea of me leaving, but she gets it. She longed for home for so long, and finally found it with her last foster home. She understands that sometimes you just want to be home. And honestly, the Wednesday prayer group, and Whitney and Kevin, Mrs. Fisher and the other ladies, even all their crazy matchmaking ways—you've all become the church community I needed. My mom finally accepted Jesus, and it's been so great to share that with her. I'm not sure I'm ready to give it all up. Plus, my dad may be stable now, but we both know that can change at any moment. We're going to need each other after he's gone."

"Have you talked to anyone else about this?"

"Other than Isabelle, no. And I'm not ready to tell my mom. That's why I said this stays between us. I'm still praying about it, and I'm not even sure what you have planned for the office space. I don't want to get anyone's hopes up if it doesn't happen."

They pulled up to the clinic.

Heath looked at his watch again. He really needed to get back to start with his patients for the afternoon, as much as he'd like to continue talking.

"Ashlynn, we'll talk about this more later, but for the record?" He gave her a small smile. "I think you'd be the perfect person to open a counseling center here. The space is yours if you want it."

Chapter 8

Ashlynn drove home after her session with Madelyn and thought more about that afternoon. She was glad she'd shared her idea with Heath. The more she thought about it and the more she prayed about it, the more she thought it was the right move.

Besides, if her dad took a turn for the worse—which she knew was inevitable—she didn't want to be leaving her mom alone. Not for a while, anyway. This seemed like a good solution on several levels.

But did she know how to run her own clinic? She knew the theory of it, but actually doing it? It was a little terrifying.

She pulled into the driveway, then bowed her head. "God," she whispered, "please give me guidance. If this is the right move, make it absolutely clear. Give me the right people to help me put it into place, and put the right patients in my path. Amen."

As she slid out of her CRV, she noticed Heath's truck was there. His truck had not been at the clinic when she'd left, and she assumed he'd just gone home. *Was everything okay with Dad?* Her heart began to pound.

"Mom?" she called as she walked inside.

"In the living room."

Ashlynn's heart settled to normal, and she smiled as she walked in to see her mother watching a baseball game. She hadn't told Heath, but it was actually her mom who'd first gotten her into watching sports in the first place. They'd watched mostly basketball while she was growing up—her mom had played on her high school team back when she was young—but she had turned her mom to baseball over the last few years.

"Who's playing?" Ashlynn asked.

"The Astros and the Rangers. Astros are leading 2-0," her mother said, not looking up from the television.

"Is Heath here? I saw his truck in the driveway."

"He's back talking to your dad. Your dad called and said he needed to talk to him right away. I have no idea what that's all about, but Heath came right over."

"Weird." Ashlynn settled on the couch to watch the game with her mom.

Awhile later, Ashlynn heard footsteps coming down the hall.

"Ann, Ashlynn?" Heath said, giving Ashlynn a small smile as he stepped into the living room. "Paul asked me to come get you. He'd like to talk to all of us together."

That more than got her attention. Ashlynn rose quickly, and they all walked back to the bedroom.

Paul was sitting up in bed a book in his lap, and a weird smile on his face.

"Paul, honey, is everything okay?" her mom asked, stepping to his bedside.

"Everything is fine," Paul said, holding up the book. She peered closer and saw it was a Bible. "I've just been talking to Doc here about this Bible he's been making me read."

"Making you?" Heath laughed.

"Fine, 'encouraging' me to read. Anyway, I wanted to let you all know that as much as I hate to admit it, a lot of what is in here makes a ton of sense."

Ashlynn thought she was going to cry. "Dad, what are you saying exactly?"

"I'm saying I finally understand what the three of you have been talking about. And, well…" He gave her mom a gruff smile and pointed skyward. "I'm ready to accept Jesus."

Now she was crying. Ashlynn looked back at Heath and noticed his eyes were wet, too. So were her mom's.

Thank you, she mouthed to Heath as her father bent his head and began to pray.

"Thanks, Dustin," Heath said into his phone two days later. "I really appreciate it. I'm sure the Wilsons will all be thrilled to get this done so quickly."

"No problem, Heath," Dustin said. "Just tell them to be at the church a little early so we can go over everything."

They hung up, and Heath headed over to the Wilson house to tell them the good news. So much had happened in the last forty-eight hours, he thought. He'd figured Ashlynn telling him she may want to move back to White Lake permanently would be the biggest, but then Paul had reached out, answering the prayer for his salvation that they'd all been wanting for so long.

Ashlynn met him at the door before he had a chance to knock. He followed her into the kitchen, where both her parents were sitting, drinking tea. It was great to see Paul out of bed, too.

"So, Doc, what did the pastor say?" Paul asked.

"I just got off the phone with him. He said that he'd be happy to fit in both your baptisms this Sunday morning," Heath said. "He said to just come to church a little early and he'll go over what will need to happen."

"Oh, Heath, thank you so much! This is perfect!" Ann said with more excitement than Heath had ever heard from her. In fact, she and Paul both looked like new people.

Heath smiled over at Ashlynn and offered his hand. "Care to take a walk?"

She just smiled and took his hand. "We'll back in a little while," she said to her parents, then let him guide her out.

They walked hand-in-hand in comfortable silence for about twenty minutes. It was still fairly warm but the trees were definitely starting to change now, fall beginning to show.

"Heath, I cannot tell you how grateful I am for everything you've done for my dad," Ashlynn said. She sounded happy, Heath realized—truly happy. "You went way above and beyond your duty as his physician, and you have no idea how much it means to me."

She was looking at him in a way he'd never seen from her before—something between admiration, respect, and pure joy.

He smiled and led her to the bench they always seemed to gravitate toward.

"You know," he said as they sat, "when Jessica died, people were always telling me things like, 'She's in a better place now,' or 'This isn't really goodbye because you'll see each other again,' or my personal favorite, 'At least she's not suffering anymore.' I'd get so frustrated with phrases like that. It didn't matter to me that she was with Jesus now, or that I'd see her again—her absence just *hurt*. It didn't matter that she wasn't suffering anymore, because I was mad she'd had to suffer at all."

"I think I understand."

He paused, thinking of how to word what he wanted to say next. "But then, when Victoria died, people weren't saying those phrases. Or if they did, they weren't true. When Jessica died, I was angry and frustrated, and I didn't want to cling to the hope that Jesus promised it wasn't really the end and I'd see her again, yet the hope was still there, underneath it all. But when Victoria died, I didn't have that hope."

They were quiet a moment. Heath added, "That's part of what made me really wake up and realize how angry and selfish I was being. Going through loss is hard, but it's a million times worse when you don't have the hope that the person you lost is now with Jesus. I promised I would continue to pray for people around me who I knew did not know Jesus, that I would do my part to share Him with them. Your dad was the first person I really got to experience that with, and I am so glad... especially because..."

His heart thudded, and he let the words just tumble out. "I'm especially glad because I know how important it is to you, too."

They were holding both of each other's hands now, and he turned to face her.

"Ashlynn, you and I both understand what it means to lose someone who didn't know Jesus. And while I would not wish that feeling upon anyone, I am glad I now have someone to share that with. Someone who understands the pain is different."

Ashlynn just looked up at him, unshed tears shining in her eyes. "I'm glad, too, to have you to share this with," she said softly. "Both the memories and pain of losing Victoria, but also the joy of getting to see my father finally come to Christ."

And then, to his utter surprise, she leaned up and gently kissed him.

Ashlynn felt a tickle in her belly as Heath deepened the kiss, and she let herself relax.

Then her mind kicked in, and she pulled back.

What are you thinking? She could not be kissing Heath Lancaster. "I—ah...." She took a deep breath, hoping to still her jitters. "I'm sorry. Heath, I—I shouldn't have done that."

She stared at her hands, cheeks burning.

Heath grabbed her shoulders and gently made her look at him. "Hey, don't apologize. I would be lying if I said I haven't thought about doing that several times in the last couple of weeks. I know we have a rocky past, and things between us have just started to be where we can trust each other, but I have to be honest—I do have feelings for you."

Ashlynn wanted to get up and run away. Heath Lancaster was telling her he had feelings for her! And in her heart she knew those feelings were not one-sided. But she should not be having these sort of feelings for Victoria's boyfriend, should she? And how could they ever have a normal relationship, given all they'd been through?

"Heath, I would be lying too if I said your feelings weren't mutual. But I don't know what to do with all this. As much as we've changed, as much as we're not the people we were in high school, those things still happened. Can we really just put everything we've been through behind us?"

"We won't know if we aren't willing to give it a try," Heath said seriously. "We can take it slow. Continue to get to know each other like we have been. We don't have to start a romantic relationship right now, but can we at least leave the possibility of that happening open?"

Ashlynn thought for a minute. Maybe he was right. Maybe despite all the odds, they could make it work. Was it at least worth a try?

"Okay," she finally said, so quietly she wasn't even sure she'd said the words aloud.

"Okay what?"

She met his gaze. "Okay, we can give this a try. But slowly."

He smiled down at her, squeezed her hands. "That sounds perfect."

Chapter 9

Heath hung up his office phone, a slice of worry snaking through him. "I'll be right there," he told Ashlynn.

Paul. He didn't remember ever hearing Ashlynn sound so worried.

He jumped in his truck and headed to the Wilsons', driving as fast as the speed limit would allow.

It was a few weeks after their walk—and their kiss. So much had happened since then: Paul had accepted Christ and been baptized, as had Ann, and Heath was now spending most of his off-hours with Ashlynn. They went to lunch most days during the week, and spent evenings with either his parents or her parents. Most evenings they ended up walking around the lake and talking. It was something he'd easily gotten used to—and if he cared to admit it, would be upset for it to end.

At the Wilsons', he raced inside without knocking and found Ashlynn in the kitchen, her eyes red.

"Hey, what's going on?" He pulled her into a hug. "What are the nurses saying?"

Wiping her eyes, she blurted, "They said they think this is it. He's barely responding. He—he's asked for you."

It was worse than he'd expected. He grabbed her hand, and they walked back into Paul's bedroom.

"Doc?" Paul said weakly.

Ann was there, too, and even though all the lights were on, the room seemed darker.

"I'm here." Paul went to him, knelt and took his hand.

"Thank you for taking good care of me, and for not giving up on me."

"Never," Heath said with a chuckle, trying not to tear up.

"One more thing," Paul said.

Paul pulled Heath close to whisper in his ear. "Take care of my little girl, okay?" His voice was rough. "I'm not stupid. I can see you two care deeply for each other. Just take care of each other. Got it?"

Heath nodded. "Yes, sir."

"Ashlynn?" Paul coughed.

"Yes, Dad?"

"I love you. I'm sorry I mocked you in high school. You were right—Jesus is worth it."

Ashlynn sniffled, but she held it together. "I'm so glad to hear that, Dad. I love you, too."

"Now, can you two leave me alone with my wife?"

They both nodded, and Heath led Ashlynn out to the living room. She turned on a baseball game but muted it, and they sat there in silence.

"Thanks for stopping by Dustin." Ashlynn heard Heath say about an hour later. The pastor was just one of the several people from the church who had stopped by, dropping off food, tissues, and even toilet paper. Most of them stayed and prayed with Ashlynn or offered a word of sympathy. Her mom had not left Paul's side the entire time, but people were understanding of that and merely told

Ashlynn to let her know they were praying for the entire family. Isabelle had called too, and told her she would be catching a flight to Houston as soon as Ashlynn let her know when the funeral services would be. It felt strange not having her best friend with her. Isabelle had been there for pretty much every event in Ashlynn's life since Victoria died. She looked over at Heath though and was glad she and her mom were not totally alone.

Heath came back inside from walking the last guest out to their car to find Ashlynn back in the living room in front of the silent baseball game. He sat down next to her and squeezed her hand. She looked up at him and gave him a sad smile and whispered "I'm glad you're here" before turning back to the television, tears in her eyes. They sat in silence for a couple of innings when Ann came into the room, crying.

"Mom?" Ashlynn sat up straight.

Ann collapsed onto the couch. "He's gone."

Heath heard a loud sob from Ashlynn, and suddenly she leapt from the couch and ran out the front door.

He looked over at Ann. He hated to leave her here alone, but he wanted to go after Ashlynn, too.

"Go," Ann said softly. "I'll be fine. She needs you."

Heath nodded and raced out the door after Ashlynn, pulling out his phone to call Mrs. Fisher as he went. He knew she would not mind coming back over and someone should be here with Ann while he tried to find Ashlynn.

Ashlynn had never been much of a runner but when she was upset, she could go quite the distance. Before she even realized it, she was back at the lake, in front of her favorite bench.

She flung herself down on the wooden seat and pulled her knees to her chest, sobbing. She buried her head. *Oh, Dad!* Her heart ached. She knew she would see her dad again, but it still just felt too soon. Why did she waste all those years being upset and angry and refusing to come back to White Lake? She would have had so much more time if she had not been so stubborn.

She sensed someone next to her and looked up to see Heath.

"How did you know where to find me?" She felt completely out of control of her emotions, which she normally did not like other people seeing. She was glad he'd come after her, however. In that moment she was more afraid of being alone than she was of being vulnerable.

"We both know the best place in White Lake." He said trying to smile. "Can I join you?"

She nodded and scooted over so he had room. "Wait! If you're here, where's my mom? I can't believe I left her at the house by herself." She said realizing how selfish she was for leaving.

"I called Mrs. Fisher. She agreed to come back to the house to sit with your mom. I knew neither one of you needed to be alone right now."

She gave him a small smile, unable to really say anything for fear of starting to cry again.

He pulled her into his arms and kissed her hair tenderly. "Look," he said. "I know those clichéd remarks about your dad being in a better place and seeing him again are annoying, but I also know they are true. Your dad found peace with Jesus before he died, and you know that makes a huge difference."

"I know." She did know. It did make all the difference. She missed her dad, truly. But knowing he was with Jesus—that helped. He wasn't gone forever. She knew she'd see him again one day.

"Thank you for everything, Heath," she said before the tears started again. "For my dad, for being here for our family, for coming to find me right now."

She let him hold her as she wept. She knew this was not really goodbye, but it still hurt.

It could have been minutes or hours, she didn't know, but finally she pulled back, spent from all the tears. They sat in silence, watching the ducks chase each other.

Eventually she realized Heath was staring at her, a mischievous look on his face.

"What?" she asked.

"What would you do if I threw you in the lake right now?" he asked.

"You wouldn't dare."

"Wouldn't I?" He picked her up.

"Heath! Put me down!" Suddenly she felt like she was five years old again, giggling like a maniac as she fought against him. "What are you doing?"

He just laughed and ran with her as though she were weightless—straight into White Lake.

She sputtered, still laughing. "You're going to pay for this, Lancaster!"

"Oh, really?" he teased before she lunged at him and pulled him down with her.

When they finally crawled back onshore, she cocked her head and smiled up at him, dripping wet.

"What was that all about?" she asked.

"I was just trying to get you to laugh again," he said, the picture of innocence. "It worked, didn't it?"

"It did. But what if it didn't?"

He grinned at her. "Then I was going to try this."

And with that, he pulled her to him and kissed her, long, tender, and sweet.

She returned the kiss, her hair wet against her back and her jeans soggy with lake water.

"That works, too," she said, pulling back to smile. It did work, she realized. She missed her dad, and she knew she always would. But she was incredibly glad she had Heath here with her.

A giggle erupted from her, and then a full-blown laugh.

"What?" Now it was Heath's turn to be confused.

"There is no way that six months ago I would have believed I was at the lake having a water fight, laughing, and kissing Heath Lancaster on the same day my dad died."

He joined her, and they slowly walked back to the house. Things sure had changed.

Chapter 10

W hat time is Isabelle supposed to get into Houston?" Heath asked from Ashlynn's parents' living room, muting the baseball game on television.

"Seven o'clock," she said, sounding distracted. She was perched on the floor in front of his chair, arms wrapped around her knees like a kid.

"So if we leave here by five that should be enough time to get there?"

"We?" She looked up.

"Well, yeah. I didn't think you wanted to drive all the way to Houston by yourself two days after your dad died. Even if you did, *I* don't want you driving to Houston by yourself two days after your dad died!"

Ashlynn got up and sat in his lap, giving him a kiss on the cheek. "Thank you. I could not do this without you."

He cupped her face and kissed her forehead. "I'll be honest, I'm not sure I could do this without you, either. I've lost patients before, but never like this."

Ashlynn looked up into his bright green eyes and smiled contently.

"Now let's see if my Rockies can beat your Astros," she said as he wrapped an arm around her and they watched the game cuddling there together.

On their drive to the Houston airport, Heath kept his eyes on the road, but his voice sounded a little nervous to Ashlynn's ears. "So exactly how much have you told Isabelle about me?" he asked.

Ashlynn smiled reassuringly. "She knows all about our history. When we first moved in together, I was still kind of a mess. She knew all about Victoria, about my feelings about how you were responsible, and about my own guilt for trusting you to get her home after I left. She knew about how I felt like my friendship with Victoria was crumbling, and that I blamed you for a lot of that, too."

Heath groaned. "So basically, she's going to hate me."

Ashlynn laughed. "Let me finish. When I first got back to White Lake, she was the first person I told about you being back, too, and treating my dad. And, believe it or not, she was actually the first one to suggest maybe I had been too hard on you, and maybe there was a reason we were put back into each other's lives. She told me I needed to give you another chance."

"So you're telling me I owe a lot to this best friend of yours?"

She chuckled. "I don't know if you've picked up on this, but if you're going to be in my life, she's a part of the deal. We've both been through a lot and, in a sense, we grew up together. College was a growing experience for both of us, and it only made our friendship that much stronger. We're like sisters. My parents are amazing, and her foster parents became the family she never had, but neither of had siblings, until we met each other."

"I know I was a big reason you and Victoria had problems. I look back at that time in my life, and I can't believe how I acted. I never want to come between friends again. It sounds like what you and

Isabelle have is even stronger than you and Victoria, and I would be an idiot if I thought I even had a chance of coming between you. I know I'd be on the losing end of that battle."

She grinned. "At least you know where you stand."

He pulled her CRV into the airport and parked, then walked around to open her door, grabbing her hand to help her out of the car. It still made her cheeks flush when their hands made contact.

They walked hand in hand to the arrivals terminals and found the right baggage claim. There they sat to wait for Isabelle, Heath's arm around her waist while she put her head on his shoulder. She liked that he didn't make her talk if she didn't want to. He was content just sitting with her. As a counselor, she often knew when someone needed to speak and when they needed to just to sit and process. She often found others did not have the same ability, but Heath was different. He always seemed to sense when she just needed it quiet. She thought back over the last few weeks. Heath had been there through everything: her dad accepting Jesus, both her parents' baptisms, her father dying. And each time it was like he sensed exactly what she needed in each moment. He was good for her, she realized. Really good.

Isabelle, when she finally arrived, was not at all what Heath had pictured. When Ashlynn had told him her best friend was a former foster child and now a high school music teacher, he pictured a shy, reserved person.

But while the woman standing before him was barely five feet tall, her energy was anything but small. She had platinum pixie-cut hair with streaks of green and purple sprinkled throughout, and she wore round, trendy glasses and a diamond stud in her nose.

"Ashlynn!"

"Isabelle!"

The girls screamed and hugged, and Heath watched, amused.

"It is so good to see you," Ashlynn said, pulling back from the hug to include Heath in the group.

"I'm so sorry about your dad, but I am glad I am finally going to get to see this town you've told me so much about. Oh, you must be Heath! I'm Isabelle." Skipping social norms, she gave him a hug, as well.

Heath stifled a laugh. "It's nice to meet you Isabelle. I've heard a lot about you."

"I've heard all about you too. Don't worry." She elbowed him. "I'm still rooting for you."

He laughed. "Good to know. Here let me take your bags. Have you eaten yet?"

"No, and I'm starving!"

Ashlynn scoffed. "What, has it been over an hour since you last ate?"

"Three, actually."

Heath shook his head at their dynamic. "Well, we haven't eaten yet either, so why don't we find someplace to go on the way back to White Lake. Isabelle, do you have a preference?"

"I'll eat pretty much anything."

"Yeah, don't let her size fool you," Ashlynn piped up as they made their way to the car. "She's totally serious."

Heath put Isabelle's luggage in the back, then opened her door as well as the passenger door for Ashlynn before getting in the driver's side.

"Wait a minute," Isabelle said from the back seat, her mouth slightly open. "You're letting Heath drive your car?"

"Um, yeah. I've been so distracted with everything that when Heath offered to come with me, I thought it would better for him to drive."

"Then why didn't you take his car?"

"I only have a truck without an extended cab." Heath said, not sure what the big deal was. "We wouldn't have all fit."

"But you never let anyone drive your car. You don't even let *me* drive it!"

Ashlynn just blushed and shrugged. Heath, however, grinned. He was glad she trusted him.

At the hamburger joint, Heath was surprised that Isabelle not only ate her entire burger but an order of onion rings and half of Ashlynn's fries, too. Isabelle was nice, and he had to admit he enjoyed seeing the two best friends together. The glimpses he had gotten over the last few weeks, of what he felt like was the real Ashlynn, he saw in full force when she was around Isabelle. He realized trying to convince Ashlynn to stay in White Lake would mean separating the two best friends. Could he really do that? He had told Ashlynn he would never come between them but that is essentially what he would be doing. But where did that leave him? He had to admit he really did not want her to go back home to Colorado.

On the drive back to White Lake. Ashlynn's exhaustion finally won. She leaned her head against the window and was snoozing before they got on the interstate.

"Is she asleep?" Isabelle said from the back seat.

"Yup, light snoring and all," he said with a chuckle.

"Good, we can talk without her listening."

Heath cocked an eyebrow, a little afraid of what Isabelle might have to say to him. "What did you want to talk about?"

"The two of you, of course. Ashlynn tells me everything, but she's been cagey where you're concerned. So, spill Doc."

Heath blinked, suddenly more than a little uncomfortable. "I'm not sure what you want me to tell you."

"Well, how about when you're going to tell her you love her, for starters?"

"Excuse me?" Heath choked out.

"Oh, come on." Isabelle waved a hand, grinning. "It's obvious to everyone except you. Well, and Ashlynn, but she's mostly in denial I'm sure."

"We've just started getting to the point that we don't hate each other. I think love is a little strong."

Isabelle scoffed. "First of all, I don't buy that you ever 'hated' her. Second, you guys went straight from barely tolerating each other to head over heels in love without anything in-between."

"Which is probably not a very smart way to start a relationship."

"I disagree," Isabelle said smugly. "I don't think you guys would ever work as friends. There is too much history and hurt. You either have to completely trust each other and use that history to shape your relationship, or decide that it's too much to overcome. I don't think anything in the middle would ever work."

"No offense, but when did you become a relationship expert?"

She just grinned at him. "You don't live with a therapist for as long as I have without picking up on a few things. So back to my question—when are you going to tell her? And, what are you going to do about it? Have you convinced her to stay in White Lake and open her own practice yet?"

Heath laughed. "You do know that if she moves to White Lake, you'll be alone in Colorado? I'm not sure I can do that to you guys."

Isabelle sighed. "Look, as much as I want to be selfish here, her moving back to White Lake for good makes sense in so many more ways than just because you live here. She's always wanted to make a difference, and owning her own practice in White Lake would do that. She's always missed being around her parents, and her mom needs her right now. She's finally able to see White Lake as her home again instead of just the place where Victoria died."

"But what about you?"

"Heath, I've been basically on my own my entire life until Ashlynn came around. Yeah, it'll be hard to break in a new roommate, but it doesn't mean we won't still be best friends."

Heath frowned, suddenly far more serious. "What if she decides she doesn't want to move?"

"Well, then you'll have to decide what that means for you. If you're going to be together, eventually one of you is going to have to move. But for the record, I think she wants to come back home. She just needs the right push."

Heath smiled at her. "Thanks, Isabelle. Oh, and just so you know, I heard a rumor that the White Lake Elementary music teacher is considering retiring at the end of this school year. Just a thought," he said, winking at her as he pulled into Ashlynn's driveway.

Chapter 11

What was is about a funeral that suddenly made her self-conscious about her wardrobe, Ashlynn wondered as she stood in her closet, surveying her clothing options. She'd never been one to care about what people thought about her clothes, but suddenly she felt like the outfit she picked for her father's funeral was supposed to somehow be a perfect symbol of her grief. She remembered feeling the same way at Victoria's funeral.

She sighed, deciding to just stick with what she and Isabelle had decided upon last night: a simple black dress with an open grey cardigan.

As she stood in the shower, hot water mingling with her tears, she thought about the last time she'd attended a funeral in White Lake. How broken and helpless she'd felt those first days after Victoria's death. *Thank you, God.* She was grateful that she did not have those same feelings today. She knew she would see her father again.

After she dressed, she walked down to the kitchen, giving a small smile when she saw her mother, Isabelle, and Heath all sitting at the table eating muffins from the diner.

"Is that a maraschino cherry in my blueberry muffin?" Isabelle asked.

Ashlynn gave a chuckle. "It must have been Kevin's day to make muffins. He insists that you can't have just a normal muffin. You have to add something to it. It drives Whitney crazy."

Heath stood and gave her a hug and a kiss on the forehead. "How are you doing this morning?"

She squeezed his hand and walked over to join everyone at the table. "I'm doing okay. I have much more peace about today than I thought I would. Thank you again, Heath, for all you did for my father before he died." She looked at her mother. "How are you, Mom?"

Heath looked at her mom with concern. "Ann, is there anything I can do before we leave for the church?"

Her mother just looked up at them, tears still evident in her eyes. "No, I think I've got everything. We should probably get going, though. I told Paul's sisters I would meet them at the church at 10:00."

Her mom started to clear her dishes, but Isabelle stood and took her plate and cup.

"Let me do that, Ann." Isabelle smiled kindly. "You go finish gathering your things and head to the car. We'll meet you out there in just a few moments."

"Thank you for being here, Belle," her mom said, wrapping Isabelle in a quick hug. "You're an important part of this family, and I'm glad you could make it."

Ashlynn smiled as she watched them. She was glad that not only could she rely on Isabelle for support, so could her mother.

After the service, Heath helped Ann, then Isabelle and Ashlynn, into one of the limousines reserved for the family to get to the cemetery after the funeral. He looked behind him to see if Ashlynn's aunts needed help getting in the other limo behind them, but saw that her uncles had it taken care of. He looked around trying to remember where he parked his truck.

"Aren't you getting in?" Ashlynn asked as he started to close the door.

"It's the family car," Heath said.

"Heath, you're basically family," Ann said.

Isabelle cocked an eyebrow. "Didn't we already have this conversation when we were going to sit in the family section in the sanctuary?" she said, a sarcastic yet playful tone in her voice.

Heath gave a small smile, then climbed in and sat on Ashlynn's left, Isabelle sitting on her right and Ann across from them. He had to admit that it felt good that they thought of him as family. Good, yet still a little strange.

The drive was short, but quiet.

"It was a nice service, Ann," Isabelle said.

"Thank you. It really was. I was pleased at the turnout."

"Me, too. Dad was an important part of the community," Ashlynn said. "Even with his cranky exterior, people could tell he really cared about the town."

At the cemetery, Heath helped each of the ladies out of the car, then continued holding Ashlynn's hand as they walked the path to where Paul's body was being buried. This gathering was much smaller, consisting of mostly just family, as well as a couple of close friends, including Mrs. Fisher and, of course, Pastor Dustin. Dustin read a short passage from the Bible and said a short prayer.

Heath watched as Ashlynn followed her aunts and mom by scooping a small pile of dirt into the grave and then placing a rose on her father's casket. She looked like she could fall over from emotion at any moment, and he put his arm around her, as much to keep her upright as to comfort her. Ashlynn gave him a grateful smile.

After the service was completely finished, Isabelle drifted over.

"Whitney and Kevin offered to have everyone come over to the diner for a meal if you're feeling up to it," Isabelle said. "But they said they totally understood if you would rather go home and be alone."

"Mom, what do you think?" Ashlynn asked.

Ann looked stronger now, less like she was going to collapse into tears and more like she was at peace, even if it was a sad peace. "I think that sounds wonderful," Ann said. "Tell them we'll meet everyone over there after we get our car."

When Isabelle walked off, Ann turned to Ashlynn. "While we're here, do you want to visit—"

"No." Ashlynn just shook her head at her mom.

"But sweetie, I just think maybe it's time."

"Not now, Mom. I want today to be about grieving my father, not dealing with anything else."

"Okay," Ann said. "If you're sure."

Heath just watched the two women. He had an idea what they were talking about—Victoria—but did not know for certain and definitely did not want to broach the topic now.

Ashlynn looked around the diner, amazed at all the people who'd come to mourn and celebrate with her and her mother. Sure, she had her community in Denver, but the people of White Lake gave community a whole new meaning.

"Coffee?" a deep voice behind her asked.

She turned to see Heath holding up a mug. "Do I ever say no to coffee?" she asked, smiling for probably the first time all day.

"That's what I was counting on. Where's Isabelle?"

"Last I saw, she was over helping Whitney refill coffees and making sure no one needed seconds on food."

"She seems to fit in well around here."

Ashlynn smiled for the second time that day. "Yes, she does! I'm glad. If I do move back here, I want her to feel like she has a place to visit for holidays and such."

"Does she spend most holidays with you?"

"Pretty much. Mom and Dad would come to Colorado for about a week and we'd spend most of the time doing all the fun Christmas things. Decorating the tree, going sledding, even convincing them to go to Christmas Eve services at our church. Isabelle's last foster family always invites her over too, and usually she stops by, but they still take in foster kids and she doesn't want to take away from their holiday."

"I'm glad you all have each other."

His phone rang then and he frowned with what looked like concern at the caller ID.

"Hang on, let me get this real quick. Mom?" he said into the receiver. "What? Calm down, I'll be right there. Have you called the ambulance? Okay, you go with him in the ambulance, I'll meet you at the hospital in Pine Grove. Yes, I'll call ahead and make sure Dr. Williams is there."

"What's wrong?" Ashlynn gazed at him. This didn't sound good.

Heath's face had paled. "My father wasn't feeling well after the service so they went home. Now he's collapsed. My mom thinks he had a heart attack. He's conscious but really weak. The ambulance was already in town at a call that didn't require transport, so they're headed to the house now to take him to the hospital in Pine Grove." He fumbled in his pocket like he was looking for his truck keys. "I've got to go meet my mom and make sure his cardiologist is there."

"Of course. Can I come with you?"

"I would love that, but are you sure? What about Isabelle?"

"Isabelle will be fine with Whitney and my mother. You've been here for me all week—now it's my turn." She gave his hand a squeeze. "Let me go tell them what's going on and we can leave."

Heath insisted on driving, and they made most of the drive in silence, holding hands tight. He couldn't help but remember just a few weeks ago when they were in the same seats, making this same drive for Ashlynn's dad. He still could not believe all that had transpired in such a short time.

He pulled into the hospital and parked in a spot right at the front that said "visiting physician parking."

"Fancy parking spot, Doc Lancaster," Ashlynn said as they walked inside.

"There are some perks to being a doctor in the next town over. Besides, Dr. Williams told me to park here."

He heard his name as they got off the elevator to the third floor cardiac unit.

"Mom." He hugged her. He could tell she was upset but trying desperately to hold it all in. "How's he doing? What are they saying?"

"He went in for an EKG, and Dr. Williams said he'd come out when he had the results," she said as she led them to a group of chairs in the waiting area. His mom gave Ashlynn a quick hug. "Thank you so much for coming, sweetheart. I'm so sorry to take you away from the funeral."

"Oh, I'm happy to be here, Lori. Can I get you some coffee or anything?" Ashlynn asked, looking like she was not sure what she was supposed to be doing.

"No, but thank you."

"Heath, Lori?" He heard a familiar voice say and looked up to see Dr. Evan Williams walking toward them, his face grave.

"Evan. How's he doing?" Heath asked.

"It was another heart attack, a massive one, but he's stable now," Evan said. "I'm afraid this time he will need open heart surgery. After looking at his EKG and heart cath results, we've determined he needs a triple bypass. I'd like to do the surgery right away."

"Does Dad know?"

"Yes. I spoke with him first. You all can go in to see him before we take him back to prep for surgery."

"Thanks." Heath turned to Ashlynn. "Evan was an attending at the hospital where I did part of my residency. He's one of the best cardiologists in the state."

Ashlynn just nodded as she followed Heath and his mother into the hospital room.

Heath took a deep breath. He wasn't sure if he was ready to see his dad hooked up to a bunch of machines. As if she could read his mind, Ashlynn squeezed his hand and gave him a reassuring look. At least he was not doing this on his own.

Chapter 12

Hours later, in the hospital waiting room, Ashlynn shut the cover on her Kindle and stretched groggily. On her phone she saw a text from Isabelle letting her know they were home from the diner, and her mom had gone directly to bed, but everything was fine if Ashlynn needed to stay at the hospital longer.

She looked at her watch. Was it really less than twelve hours since her father's funeral? This day seemed like it would last forever.

Heath's mom, Lori, was sound asleep in the chair next to her. Lori seemed to be taking everything fairly well, which Ashlynn thought was impressive. In fact, neither she nor Heath seemed all that surprised by the turn of events. It was almost like they'd expected this.

What had the doctor said? "This time he will need surgery." The thought bothered Ashlynn. Had Frank been sick a while? Why hadn't Heath mentioned it to her? She looked over at him, scrolling sleepily through his phone. It would explain why Frank was retiring so early, as well as why Heath hadn't been hesitant to come back to White Lake to take over the practice. But why keep it a secret? After everything she had shared with him, why not tell her the real reason he'd come back home?

Footsteps sounded, and she looked up to see Dr. Williams walking toward them.

Ashlynn nudged Heath and gently shook Lori to wake her.

"Dr. Williams," Lori said, rubbing her eyes. "Is he out of surgery?"

"Yes. The surgery went well and we've got him in a recovery room. It will be a little while before you'll be able to see him, but he's doing really well."

Heath breathed a sigh of relief next to Ashlynn, and she reached for his hand.

"Thanks, Evan. There's no one else I'd want operating on my dad. I appreciate it."

A couple of hours later, Heath pulled up to Ashlynn's parent's house and walked her to the front door. "Thank you again for coming with me. I know you had a lot on your mind today and I appreciate it."

"It's not a problem Heath." Ashlynn said, the exhaustion of the day starting to catch up to her.

He just smiled at her. "Go get some sleep. I'll see you tomorrow okay?"

She gave him a hug and quick kiss and headed inside.

"Hey, how's Heath's dad?" Isabelle said from the couch as Ashlynn walked inside.

"He's doing okay. He's stable and will make a full recovery. Why aren't you in bed?"

"I wanted to make sure you were okay. To say today has been a long day would be an understatement."

"That's sweet. But I'm fine. Go to bed, we can talk in the morning."

"If you're sure." Isabelle said, an unbelieving tone in her voice.

"I'm sure. All I want to do is sleep."

Isabelle looked liked she wanted to say more but instead she gave her a hug and walked back down the hallway to the guest bedroom. Ashlynn followed her silently. She would wait until she got some sleep to process everything that had happened.

Heath's phone beeped, jerking him out of his deep sleep. He rolled over and looked at his clock. Nine o'clock. When was the last time he'd slept that late? He picked up his phone and smiled when he saw a text from Ashlynn.

Ashlynn: Good morning! Are you going back to the hospital this morning?

Heath: Good morning to you, too. Yes, after breakfast. Are you showing Isabelle around White Lake today?

Ashlynn: As long as you don't need me to go with you.

Heath smiled. Even with everything she had been through the last few days, she still thought of him and his family. It was a weird but nice feeling to have someone wanting to take care of him for a change.

Heath: No, I'll be fine. Spend some time with your best friend.

Ashlynn: Thank you for understanding. Want to get breakfast at the diner before you leave? Isabelle isn't even awake yet ;).

Heath: Sounds great. See you in twenty minutes.

He climbed out of bed and got ready quickly. A part of him was sad Ashlynn was not going to the hospital with him, but the other part was glad her friendship with Isabelle was so important to her. He meant what he said about not wanting to come between them. Plus, he liked that she had people in her life other than him that she depended on. His job could be demanding and, honestly, he needed a wife who understood that sometimes he would not be able to drop everything for her. He wanted to protect and do anything he could for her, but he also needed someone independent enough not to fall apart if they didn't spend every minute together....

He stopped himself. *Wife*. Was he really thinking about a wife? None of his past relationships since Victoria had gotten far enough for him to even think about marriage. And he and Ashlynn had only really been dating, if you could call it that, for a few weeks. He wasn't even sure she was going to be sticking around White Lake.

And yet he had to admit he was thinking of marriage in spite of that. Ashlynn was the kind of woman who would be a perfect wife. He'd known this thing with her was serious from the moment he'd started thinking about her as "Ashlynn" and not as "Victoria's best friend" or "Paul's daughter." He thought about her constantly.

But did she feel the same way?

He shook his head. *Stop, Heath*. Her father's funeral was yesterday. His father just had open-heart surgery. They'd have plenty of time to sort through all this when they were not both in crisis mode.

Ashlynn wasn't at the diner yet when Heath walked in.

"Heath, how's your dad?" Kevin called out from behind the counter.

"Doing okay," Heath said. "He has a long recovery ahead of him, but he was very fortunate to not have more damage than he did."

"I'm so glad to hear it. We were all really worried once word got out." Kevin grabbed a paper bag and two coffee cups and passed them over the counter to Heath.

"What's this?" Heath asked, confused.

"Ashlynn called a few moments ago and placed an order to go. She said to give it to you when you showed up and tell you to meet her at the lake."

"Oh, thanks." Heath reached for his wallet.

But Kevin waved it away. "On the house. Between your father's surgery and Ashlynn's dad dying, the least we can do is feed you. I think Whitney stuck a few extra muffins in there to take to Ann and Isabelle, too."

"Thanks, man, I really appreciate it."

"No problem. Tell your dad we're all praying for him."

Heath nodded and took the bag to his truck. Once there, he glanced in the bag and smiled when he saw his favorite breakfast sandwich. Though they'd only eaten breakfast together a few times, Ashlynn had picked up on what his favorite was. His coffee was the way he liked it, too: cream, no sugar. He liked that she noticed the little details.

At the lake, he parked his truck and smiled as he saw Ashlynn already sitting at their bench.

"I see Kevin gave you my message?" she said as he walked up. "I figured a breakfast lake picnic was better than sitting in the diner with half the town staring at us."

Heath laughed and sat down. "I guess the golden child and the former bad boy is a compelling story."

"More like the son who came to help his dad and the long-lost daughter who can't get over the past."

The way she said it made him cock his head at her. "You okay? Seems like you have something on your mind."

She bit her lip and sighed. "Can I ask you something?"

He frowned. "Of course."

"What did Dr. Williams mean when he said it was 'another' heart attack and that 'this time' he would need surgery? Has your dad been sick awhile?"

That was what was bothering her? "He had a mild heart attack a couple of years ago. Dr. Williams said he thought a lot of it was due to stress and that he needed to take it easy."

"So that's why he retired early? That's why you moved here?"

"The four of us—Dr. Williams, me, and my parents—thought him retiring was in his best interests. He didn't want to leave his practice to just anyone, so I offered to move here and take over. Honestly, it was the best decision for me, anyway." Heath meant that. If he really thought about it, other than quitting football to go to medical school, he could not think of a decision that was made a bigger impact on him for the better.

Ashlynn was quiet for a long moment. Then she asked in a small voice, "Why didn't you tell me?"

Heath was not sure how to answer. "I guess we thought by reducing his stress, changing his diet, and adding some heart medication, he'd be fine. He didn't want to worry everyone when he didn't think it was a big deal."

Ashlynn's face fell. "I understand why you didn't tell *everyone*. But why didn't you tell me? We're supposed to be learning to trust each other. How can I trust you when you keep secrets from me?"

Heath was confused. Did she really think he purposefully kept this from her? It was not like they had even really talked about his dad, or why he moved to back to White Lake. He was not trying to keep her in the dark, it just never came up.

"Secrets? It's not like I was intentionally keeping this from you, Ashlynn. I just didn't think it was a big deal. You can trust me because I've been nothing but honest with you." A sliver of anger began, but he kept it back. He knew she was only upset because she cared, but still.

"I didn't say you haven't been honest, but you keep so much of yourself closed off." Her cheeks were pink now. "You want me to move my entire life here, but I'm not even sure I know who you really are. You want me to trust you, but you won't do the same."

"I told you about Jessica! What else do you thinking I'm keeping from you?"

She closed her eyes a moment, then opened them and looked straight at him. "What really happened the night Victoria died?" She asked quietly. "Why did you leave instead of bring her home?"

This was ridiculous. He stood up. "You know what happened, Ashlynn. I offered to take her home." He could hear how cold his voice sounded, but he suddenly didn't care anymore. "I got tired of waiting for her and left. End of story."

Just go. You should be at the hospital with your dad, not having a stupid fight.

And giving her one last look, he turned and started back to his truck.

"Hey!" Ashlynn said as Heath turned and walked away. She ran after him. "I'm not done talking to you!"

She jumped in front of him, fully mad now. This was not how she wanted to have this conversation, but it was a conversation that needed to happen.

"Don't think for a minute that I buy that you just got tired of waiting. The man I've gotten to know over the last few weeks would never do something like that. What really happened?"

His jaw was tight. "I'm not the same person now that I was then, Ashlynn." His words were clipped. "I was an angry, selfish kid back then who didn't care enough about his girlfriend to make sure she got home safely."

"But you are the same person! Looking back, I saw glimpses of it at that party, even! The angry kid who wanted to party and act selfish? That was never the real you, Heath. I know there is more to the story." Angry tears filled her eyes. "I—I just wish you trusted me enough to tell me!"

Heath looked down at his shoes, then slowly met her eyes. "I'm sorry, Ashlynn, but no. I just can't."

She took a deep breath, trying not to give into the tears. *Can't, or won't?* She spent years believing the worst in him but now she knew there had to be more to the story. It took a lot to admit she had been wrong, and stubborn all these years. Clearly that was not enough for him to fully trust her. Maybe he had not forgiven her after all.

"Then I'm sorry, too, Heath. I'm sorry, because whatever this thing is between us, I don't think it's going to work out. I need someone who can trust me one hundred percent, even with the hard stuff."

He looked like he had been punched in the stomach. Ashlynn started to take it back but Heath interrupted her before she had the chance, his voice almost sounding like a completely different person, "I guess you were right all along. There's just too much history to make this work."

This time, when he walked off, she let him.

Chapter 13

Heath spent most of the drive to Pine Grove Hospital alternating between feelings of anger and sadness. By the time he got to his father's new room at the hospital, he was pretty firmly set on the angry side of his emotions—something he apparently did not hide well from his mother.

"Heath, what is wrong with you?" She whispered, following him out to the waiting room. "You've been snippy with everyone today! I'm about to send you home!"

He let out a deep breath. "I'm sorry, Mom. Ashlynn and I had a huge fight before I came here, and whatever sort of relationship we had is over before it ever really began. I'm sorry to take it out on all of you."

His mother sat down next to him. "Oh, honey. What was the fight about?"

Heath sighed. "She was upset that I didn't tell her sooner about Dad's health. She said it just proved I keep secrets from her and that I don't trust her."

"She didn't know before last night?" His mother sounded surprised.

"I didn't think it was that big of a deal. It wasn't like I intentionally tried to hide it."

"I know that. I just think it's a little strange you never told her, is all. I assumed when she was with you last night that she knew everything. Now surely that wasn't the only thing to derail your relationship?"

He sighed again. "She also asked me what really happened the night Victoria died."

"Oh, Heath. You know you're going to have to tell her the whole story one day." His mom put her hand on his shoulder.

"Mom, it's not my story to tell. And besides, it doesn't matter. I left Victoria at the party. Her only way home was with someone who'd been drinking, and because of that, she died. That's the only part of the story that matters."

"Maybe you should let Ashlynn decide that for herself."

As he watched his mom rise and walk back to his father's room, he wondered if she was right.

"Why does my bag say 'Just Craftin' Around' while the sign out front says 'Craft Around the Corner'?" Isabelle asked as they left the craft store and headed toward the diner.

Ashlynn gave a weak smile. "That craft store has had probably thirty different names since it opened. The owners see some cutesy name somewhere and decide that must be the name for the store. Then a few months later, they find another one. It's a never-ending cycle."

"Man, I love this place! I'm seriously going to have to visit you all the time!"

"You mean *if* I move here. I'm not even sure that's going to happen."

"Now you're just being silly. First of all, I'm pretty sure you're blowing this whole thing with Heath out of proportion." She stopped and Ashlynn hoped her "stay out of it look" was working. "Okay, we won't go there." Isabelle said and Ashlynn was relieved. "However," she started hesitantly, "didn't you say he wasn't the only reason you were thinking about moving? Whatever else might or might not be happening between you two doesn't change that."

"Except I want to rent out the offices next to where Heath works. I'm not sure where we stand now, but I'm pretty sure we are not on 'rent me your office space' terms."

"You guys will figure it out. Ash, you belong here. I felt that from our phone conversations, but now that I'm here, it's undeniable. This is where you are supposed to be!"

"Belle, how can you be so sure? And why are you so eager to get rid of me anyway?" Ashlynn said a little put off by her friend's persistence.

Isabelle's eyes filled with tears. "Of course I don't want you to move. I get sad just thinking about it. But I can just tell—this is exactly where you are supposed to be, Ashlynn. Your father just died, you've been truly heartbroken for maybe the first time ever, and you've been forced to face a past you've been avoiding for a decade. And yet despite all this, I've never seen you look more content! I feel it deep inside my soul. And who am I to stand in the way of that?" Isabelle's voice broke on the last, and the two friends hugged.

"But what will you do?" Ashlynn asked. "I can't leave you all alone. We promised we would never do that to each other."

"You wouldn't be leaving me all alone. I have other friends. I'll find another roommate. It won't be the same, but I'll survive. Yes, we promised we wouldn't abandon each other, but we also promised we would always make sure the other person followed what God was calling them to. Even it if means one of us ends up living across the world in Africa or something. Remember? White Lake might be far away from Denver, but it's certainly not as far away as Africa."

"Thanks, Belle." They hugged again.

"That's what I'm here for," Isabelle said as they approached the diner, then said with a smirk, "Plus, you never know. I like it here, and I hear the elementary music teacher is thinking of retiring. Maybe I'll just move with you."

"What? How did you hear that?"

"A little birdie told me. A handsome doctor-birdie." Isabelle said laughing as she opened the diner door.

"Hey Ashlynn and Isabelle!" Whitney called out from the counter, waving as Ashlynn and Isabelle slid into an empty booth. "I'll be right with you to get your order. Want to start with two Cherry Cokes and some onion rings?"

"See?" Isabelle told Ashlynn. "I've been going to the same café in Denver for two years, and no one even remembers my face much less my name. I've been here three days and they not only know my name but my favorite drink and junk food."

Ashlynn rolled her eyes. "Most people probably pick up on your love of Cherry Coke and onion rings pretty quickly."

"Ashlynn?" She heard a woman say, and she looked up to see Heath's mom approach their table.

"Lori? Hi!" Had Heath told his mom? She felt her chest begin to tighten.

"I'm sorry to interrupt your lunch," Lori said warmly. "And you must be the Isabelle I've been hearing so much about."

"Like I said." Isabelle winked at Ashlynn. "Everyone knows me already!"

Ashlynn ignored her and smiled at Lori. "Yes, Isabelle is my best friend and my roommate in Denver. Isabelle, this is Lori Lancaster, Heath's mother."

"It's nice to meet you." Isabelle sat up straighter, giving Ashlynn a significant look.

"So Lori, how's Frank doing?" Ashlynn cut Isabelle off before she could say something embarrassing.

"He's recovering pretty well. Ah, can I sit down a sec?" She scooted in next to Ashlynn, her voice low. "Look, sweetie, I don't want to get in between whatever is or isn't happening with you and Heath, but I know my son, and he can be extremely stubborn."

Ashlynn gave a rueful smile and nodded for her to continue.

Lori gave her a kind look. "Do I assume correctly that you'll be heading to Houston to take Isabelle back to the airport in the next few days?"

Ashlynn nodded. "Yes. She leaves tomorrow."

Lori slid a small spiral notebook and a pen from her purse and jotted something down, passed it over. "Can you do me a favor while you're there? There's someone I want you to go see. I think maybe she can help you understand a little bit about where Heath is coming from."

"You know, I pride myself on being a pretty empathetic doctor, but not until now have I fully appreciated what the patient feels while sitting in this boring, sterile place we call a hospital," Heath's dad said as they were sitting in his hospital room watching a movie.

"I know. I was thinking it's been a long time since I've spent this much time in one room in a hospital," Heath said, thinking of his sister.

"Almost fifteen years," Frank said sadly.

"It's hard to believe it's really been that long."

"Yet at the same time, so much has happened since then. Heath, I'm sorry us moving here after Jessica's death was so hard on you. I still fully believe it was the best move for our family, but maybe we should have listened to your concerns more and tried harder to help you in the transition."

"Dad, it's fine. Really. You and Mom were grieving, too, and you're right—it was the best decision for our entire family. I don't think I would be the man I am today if we had stayed in Houston."

"You've become quite the man, son. I couldn't be prouder of you."

"Thanks, Dad."

"Okay, enough of this mushy talk. Hand me that remote and let's see if we can find a game or something."

Heath chuckled and flipped through the channels, finally landing on a baseball game. He frowned, thinking about Ashlynn. Was this what it was going to be like now? Thoughts of her, or things she liked, making him feel heartbroken? They were never officially a couple, and it had only been a few weeks. How could he possibly be missing her this much?

"Am I interrupting anything?" A voice came from the doorway.

Heath looked up to see Pastor Dustin standing there.

"Come on, in pastor," Frank said, smiling. "It's nice of you to come."

"Everyone at the church has been praying for you, Frank. How are you doing?" Dustin sat in the chair on the other side of the bed.

"I'm doing okay. They say I'll have a long rehabilitation period, but I'm fortunate to still be alive. I can handle a little rehab."

Heath tried not to laugh. Not known to be a very patient person, the idea of his father being fine with rehab was comical.

When Dustin went to leave about a half-hour later, Heath saw him out.

"Thanks for coming, Dustin," Heath said as they approached the front door. "It means a lot."

"It's no problem. I just wish we knew he was sick earlier. I feel like we could have done more to help before it got this serious, or at least been praying."

"We just didn't want to make a big deal out it. We were fine—really."

Dustin paused for a moment, looking at Heath like he wanted

to say something. Then he walked to a bench and sat, motioning for Heath to sit next to him.

Heath did, curious.

"My late wife, Emily, had one of the strongest spiritual gifts of mercy that I've ever seen. She would literally feel people's pain when they were going through something difficult. She would be up at night just burdened for the world." Dustin shook his head. "I remember shortly after Charlotte was born, we found out some friends had experienced several miscarriages. They didn't tell anyone until one of them resulted in the wife needing surgery, and her husband needed someone to help take her to the hospital. We were all shocked and devastated for them, but Emily was also upset. She said 'how am I supposed to mourn with those who mourn if I don't know about it?'"

Heath nodded. He knew what Dustin was trying to say. In hindsight, it seemed strange that they'd gone to such lengths to conceal his dad's heart attack.

"Heath, Emily was right. God calls us to weep with those who weep, but too often, we think we need to do things on our own. Not only do we cheat ourselves of letting the body of Christ lift some of the burden, but we cheat the body of Christ of getting to do what we're called to do. I saw that on full display when Emily died suddenly of a brain aneurysm. The same people she walked beside during their grief came to Charlotte's and my aid when we needed it. It's part of what being a part of a church body is all about."

Heath pondered that for a moment, and his mind filled with the look of hurt and betrayal on Ashlynn's face. Was that what Ashlynn had meant when she'd said she needed him to trust her? She wanted to help carry his burdens?

He had never really thought of it that way but he supposed that is what being in a relationship, being partners, looked like. He now realized why she got so upset. It was not just that she felt like he did not trust her, he was basically telling her that he did not need her. *Wow, what a jerk move.* He definitely had some things to think about.

"Thanks, Dustin. I think I needed that more than you know."

Chapter 14

The next day, Ashlynn took a deep breath as she walked up the steps of an old but renovated Victorian house in Houston. Saying a quick prayer for strength, she pulled open the door of the Sunnyhaven Treatment and Rehabilitation Center.

"May I help you?" A young woman asked at the reception desk.

"I have an appointment to see Courtney Anderson." Ashlynn said as she took in her surroundings. The building had a feel about that felt equal parts clinical and homey. She wondered how long Courtney had lived here. With all the time and energy she spent blaming Heath for Victoria's accident, she hated to admit she had not really given the other person responsible for the accident a whole lot of thought. Her stomach turned thinking about how she would react when she saw her.

"Are you Ashlynn Wilson?" The young woman asked, and Ashlynn nodded. "I just need to see your ID and have you fill out this visitor's form."

Ashlynn handed over her driver's license and filled out the requested form.

"Thanks. Ms. Anderson said to bring you right in, so if you'll just follow me."

Ashlynn smiled at the girl and followed her down the hall to an office that said "Manager" on the door.

"Ms. Anderson? Ms. Wilson is here to see you."

Ashlynn tried to hold back a gasp as she saw the unmistakable red hair and petite features of Courtney Anderson sitting behind the desk.

"Thanks, Rachel. Ashlynn, I'm so glad you agreed to come," Courtney said kindly, gesturing to the chair with a smile as the receptionist left the room and closed the door. "Have a seat."

Ashlynn sat down and cleared her throat. "Uh, thanks. I have to be honest, when Lori Lancaster suggested I come visit you at a treatment and rehab center, this is not what I was expecting."

"You expected me to be one of the residents, right?" Courtney gave a mischievous smile.

"Guilty. Why didn't you tell me when I called and asked to meet with you?"

"I wasn't sure you'd really come, for one, and I didn't really want to answer a lot of questions on the phone. Ashlynn, I have to say I was really glad when Lori called me and said she'd told you to contact me." Courtney looked shy now. "I've wanted to talk to you about what really happened the night Victoria died and the events that followed for years, but I'd heard you'd started over in Colorado, and I—well, I didn't want to interrupt your life with old memories and heartache. I appreciate you coming here and hearing me out. Do you want a drink before I get into it? I have coffee, tea, water?"

"Uh, yeah, coffee would be great." Ashlynn said, still trying to take all this new information in. She honestly had not thought about what she expected out of this meeting, but seeing Courtney as the manager of a treatment facility, seemingly doing pretty well for herself, was definitely not it.

"Cream or sugar?" Courtney asked, pouring them cups from a small coffee pot by the window.

"Just black is fine."

"Something we have in common." Courtney smiled again, handing her a mug and taking a second one back around to sit behind her desk. "Look, I know this is weird. But like I said, I am glad you're here."

"Well, I guess go ahead then." *Say what it is you've been wanting to say to me all these years.* She gritted her teeth and forced herself to stay calm. Being here was a lot harder than she'd expected.

"Thank you. Do you mind if we pray first, though? I'm nervous."

Ashlynn just blinked, unsure she'd heard correctly. Pray? Courtney?

Courtney laughed. "I know, that's part of the story. I promise I'll get to it."

"Well, then sure, go ahead." Ashlynn bowed her head.

"Dear Father, thank You so much for bringing Ashlynn here after all these years. Thank You for redemption and second chances. Fill this place with Your presence and give me the words to say what has been on my heart for years. We love You and, again, thank you for this opportunity. It's in Your son's name we pray. Amen."

Ashlynn said a silent amen and then looked at Courtney, who seemed a lot more nervous now.

"Okay, so I guess I'll just start from the beginning, and you can stop me if you have any questions. After you left the party that night, Victoria and I kept drinking, and eventually we got pretty drunk. Then some college guys showed up with drugs and the party started to really get out of control. Heath decided we should leave before the police came and we all got in huge trouble. But Victoria and I had no desire to leave. I was still upset over my stupid breakup with Brad, and I think Victoria was more upset about you leaving to go to Colorado than she would admit, and we both just wanted a night to forget about everything. Now I was pretty drunk, so I don't remember everything, but I do remember that Heath kept trying to convince us to come with him, and finally he and Victoria got in a huge fight. She was really worked up and was trying to push Heath away while he tried to convince her to leave." Courtney paused, sighed. "She tripped and fell down the stairs. She was pretty banged up. When Heath tried to help her, she said if he didn't leave her alone and let her stay, she'd go to the police and say he'd hit her."

"Oh, Victoria," Ashlynn whispered. She loved her childhood friend, but Victoria did know how to be manipulative. "Weren't there people at the party who saw what really happened? Surely the police would have figured out the truth."

Courtney shook her head. "Nobody else was really paying attention, and I'm not proud of this, but I backed her up and said I would tell the police the same thing. The University of Texas football team had a no-tolerance policy on violence and Heath would have been kicked off the team if there was even a chance the allegations were true. I even threatened to call the police myself, and Heath finally left, telling her to call him and he would come back and get her."

Ashlynn sat frozen for a few moments. Football was the one thing that was normal for Heath after Jessica had died. He'd been young, and probably scared. It made sense he'd want to hold onto it no matter what. She took a sip of her coffee, trying to steady the thoughts swirling through her mind. "So what happened next?"

Courtney cleared her throat. "Honestly, I don't remember a lot of the rest of the night. I briefly remember running into Brad and finally convincing Victoria it was time to leave. She'd had more to drink than I, and since it was my car anyway, I decided to drive. I knew it was stupid, but neither of us lived that far away, and there were never any other cars out that late. What was the worst that could happen?"

Courtney paused, obviously collecting herself. When she looked at Ashlynn, her eyes were filled with tears. "I still don't know what happened to cause the accident itself except that we hit a tree. All I remember is waking up in the hospital and being arrested the next morning."

The counselor in Ashlynn compelled her to get up and put a hand on her shoulder, handing her a tissue.

"So how did you end up here?" Ashlynn asked in a soft voice.

"When I went to court, I took a plea bargain and the judge agreed to a three-year sentence for intoxication manslaughter. I was released after two years for good behavior but had to commit to three hundred hours of community service. While I was in prison, I wrote three letters: one to Victoria's parents, one to Heath, and one to you."

"You wrote to me? In prison?"

"Yes. I sent it to your parents' house hoping they would forward it to you. I received a response from your dad telling me to never attempt to contact you again." Courtney met her eyes. "So I didn't."

Ashlynn didn't know how she felt about that. Her dad had kept it a secret from her all those years. Why? "What did the letters say?"

"In each one I said that I was deeply sorry, that I didn't expect your forgiveness but I wanted to apologize anyway."

"Did anyone respond?"

"Victoria's parents wrote back and said that they forgave me but that they did not want to see me or hear from me ever again, that it was too painful. I heard they moved shortly after that."

Ashlynn nodded. "My mom said they moved to be near her mother's family in Nebraska about a year after her death. Nobody in White Lake has heard from them in several years."

"I don't blame them."

Ashlynn hesitated before asking her next question. "Did Heath respond?"

Courtney smiled as if she knew more than she was letting on. "I sent the letter to his parents as well, again hoping they would pass it on to him. Instead, one day a guard comes by and tells me I have a visitor. I walk to the receiving area and there I see Lori Lancaster on the other side of the glass. She told me she wanted to throw my letter away, but something had stopped her. She said she felt like it was God Himself telling her to come see me—to give me a chance to tell my story. So she did."

"Oh, wow!"

"Exactly. I was a wreck when she came. I know you were Victoria's best friend, but Victoria was mine. I just felt so guilty about what had happened. All I could do was own what I'd done. I told her what had really happened. I told her everything was my fault and that Heath had nothing to do with it. And then she did something I will never forget."

"What was that?" Ashlynn asked unable to help herself.

"She said she forgave me." Courtney smiled, tears glistening. "More than that, she said she would pray for me. And told me that God wanted to forgive me, too. I didn't really believe her, but she told me she would keep praying for me. She gave me a Bible, told me to read it, and said she would be back in a week."

"Did you read it?"

"I did! Lori came back every week for the rest of the time I was in prison. She was the only visitor I had. My parents turned their back on me after I got arrested, and I had no friends to speak of anymore. No one wanted anything to do with the girl responsible for the death of the head cheerleader. No one except Lori. Every week, she'd tell me to read a certain passage, and then the next week we'd talk about it. Eventually I started to see what you had been talking about all that time in high school. Jesus was the real deal. He forgave me for my deepest sins, even the ones that resulted in the death of a friend. Once I accepted him, I realized I wanted to do something worthwhile with my life."

"And that's how you ended up managing this place?"

"Yes. I was assigned to this place for my community service hours after I was released on parole. I worked the front desk, just like Rachel is doing now. The manager at the time, a woman by the name of Diane, took me under her wing. She encouraged me to go to school and use my story to help others, so I did. I got my bachelor's degree in communications, and then got a master's in business administration. I was hoping to find a job at a similar facility when she announced she was retiring and wanted me to take her place. I also travel some, speaking at high schools about the dangers of teenage drinking and especially of drinking and driving."

A knock on the door sounded.

"Ms. Anderson?" Rachel peeked her head in the door.

"Yes, Rachel, what is it?"

"You're needed in the west bathroom. The plumber is fixing the leaking sink and has a question for you. He said it's important."

"Tell him I'll be right there. Ashlynn, I'll be right back." Courtney followed Rachel out.

Ashlynn sat there, staring at Courtney's now empty chair. She never would have expected any of this. Courtney Anderson, one of the biggest party girls there was, the girl responsible for Victoria's death, had come to know Jesus and was running a place like this?

What surprised her even more, though, were her own feelings. She should be angry, livid even. Courtney and Victoria had manipulated Heath and, as a result, not only did Victoria die, but people blamed Heath for her death.

But Ashlynn didn't feel angry. If she were honest, she felt joy and pride, but also confusion—joy that Courtney had found a relationship in Christ, and pride that she had turned such a terrible situation into a way to help other struggling teens. They were not so different in that way. Both of them had turned a tragedy into a way to help others facing similar things.

Just as Heath had used his feelings over his sister's disease and death to motivate him to become a doctor and help others. The thought washed over her.

The confusion came from what this meant. All this time, she'd viewed Heath as the enemy. She'd resented him for a decade for something that was not really his fault. As much as she wanted to blame Courtney for that, too, that part was solely on her.

God called for forgiveness no matter the circumstances, and finding out that he was not really responsible should not matter, Ashlynn knew. She should have forgiven him a long time ago regardless.

"Sorry about that," Courtney said coming back into the office.

"That's okay. Look, Courtney, thank you for telling me your story. For what it's worth, I do forgive you for what happened."

"Thank you, Ashlynn. That means a lot. Now can I give you some advice?"

Ashlynn nodded, not sure where this was going.

"Give Heath a fair chance."

"I don't know what you're talking about," Ashlynn said defensively.

"You forget, I still talk to Lori Lancaster on an almost weekly basis. I know things." Courtney winked. "Plus, every time I mention his name, you get this look on your face that's a combination of admiration and frustration."

"It's just so complicated…"

"No, it isn't. Look, the Lancasters are some of the best people I know. It took Heath the longest, but eventually he also forgave me for what happened. He even came to check on me periodically when he lived here in Houston. However, even though he's forgiven me for what happened, a part of him still blames himself for his perceived role in what happened."

Ashlynn frowned. "But he was in an impossible situation. I'm sure I would have done the same thing."

"Then you need to tell him that," Courtney said firmly." If I know Heath, your opinion matters more than anyone's."

Ashlynn sighed. "He doesn't want to talk about it. I can't support him if he's not willing to be open about it."

Courtney gave a comforting smile. "If I've learned anything about Heath over the last few years, it's that he's super protective about those he cares about. He probably felt like he was protecting his father by not telling you about his heart condition, and he probably felt like he was protecting Victoria's memory by not telling you what really happened. I've also figured out he also thinks he has to do everything on his own. Ashlynn, talk to him. Tell him that you want to support him. And remember, you have to be patient. He's not going to change overnight."

"Thanks for being willing to tell me the truth, Courtney. This was a brave thing you did."

"Thank you. If I want people to learn anything from my story, it's that while you have to live with the consequences of your actions, you don't have to be defined by them. With Jesus, second chances are always possible. And Ashlynn, that's true of relationships, too."

Ashlynn just smiled as she told Courtney goodbye and exchanged information so they could stay in touch.

She certainly had a lot to think about on her drive back to White Lake.

In the hospital, Heath and his dad waited expectantly as Evan Williams finished the examination.

Evan smiled as he looked at them. "Everything is looking good, Frank. Unless anything major changes, you should be able to go home tomorrow. You'll need to come back about once a week for cardiac rehabilitation, but all of that can be done as an outpatient."

"Glad to hear it!" Heath's dad grinned. "I'm ready to get out of here."

Evan laughed. "So are you planning on returning to work at all, or will your retirement become official?"

"He's officially retiring. And don't even argue, Dad," Heath said when his father tried to interrupt him. "We discussed this. Your patients will understand, and I can handle the workload."

"So I guess that means I'll probably be seeing more of you, then? You'll be taking over his monthly round here, too?" Evan asked.

"That's the plan, yes," Heath said as his phone rang.

He looked at the display and his heart did a sad somersault as he saw the picture he had set for Ashlynn's contact appear on the screen. It was a candid shot of her sitting on the bench at the lake, writing in her journal. "I'm sorry, I should really take this."

He excused himself to the hallway. It was now or never, he supposed. "Hello?"

"Heath? It's Ashlynn."

Like he did not remember the sound of her voice. "Yes, I know. Is everything okay?"

He could hear her take a deep breath. "Yeah, um, I was wondering if we could meet to talk? I don't like how we left things, and before I head back to Denver next week I wanted to see you."

So she was going back to Denver. He should not be surprised. Still, the news made him feel even worse.

"Yeah, I'm in Pine Grove right now at the hospital. Do you want to meet at the lake around four? That'll give me enough time to wrap things up here and get there."

"That sounds great. I'll see you there."

He looked at his watch—he had about three hours. He prayed he would be ready for whatever she had to say.

Chapter 15

Ashlynn parked her car in the lot near the lake and took a deep breath. Grabbing the coffees she'd picked up at the diner, she headed toward the bench. Fifteen minutes till Heath was supposed to be there.

She decided to spend some time in prayer before he showed up. Popping her headphones in, she set her phone to play her worship playlist. She was lost in the music and her conversation with God when she suddenly felt a tap on her shoulder. Heath. Her heart did a slow dance.

"Ashlynn? You did say four o'clock, right?" Heath said, caution evident in his voice.

"Sorry! I got here a little early and decided to spend a little quiet time praying. I lost track of time. Thank you for agreeing to meet me. Coffee?" She asked handing him one of the insulated to-go mugs.

"Thanks." He took a drink and winced. "Ugh, I think I got yours. That's disgusting."

"No, that's what coffee really tastes like. What you drink is caffeinated cream." She grinned. At least they were still able to joke around with each other.

He sat down, and she turned to him.

"Heath, I really am glad you came. I wanted to apologize for getting so upset the other day. I should have known you had your reasons for not wanting people, even me, to know about your dad's health. We've only been getting to know each other a few weeks, and I shouldn't expect you to be able to trust me with your entire life just yet."

Heath looked sad. "I appreciate your apology, but you weren't wrong. I tend to want to do everything on my own. It isn't a healthy way to live."

"Hey, that's supposed to be my line," she joked.

Nervous energy coursed through her, and she stood and motioned for Heath to follow. Slowly they began the path, sipping their coffees as they walked.

"I'm also sorry for pressuring you to tell me about what happened the night Victoria died," Ashlynn said softly. "I understand you were trying to protect her memory."

"What are you talking about?" he asked looking confused.

She stopped walking for a minute and looked down. "When I was in Houston dropping Isabelle off at the airport, I made a stop. At Sunnyhaven."

"Sunnyhaven? You went to see Courtney?" His tone carried either indignation or confusion, Ashlynn could not tell which.

"Your mother suggested I go talk with her."

Heath sighed. "Of course she did. My mother is incapable of staying out of my love life."

Ashlynn chuckled. "For the record, I'm glad she did. Heath, not only did I deserve to know the truth, but you deserve to not feel so responsible for what happened. Victoria put you in an impossible situation."

"But I still left," he said, bowing his head.

Ashlynn took a deep breath before speaking softly. "Heath, listen to me. Even if she hadn't put you in a difficult position, the fact of the matter is, Victoria chose to get into a car with someone who had been drinking. Have you forgiven Courtney for what happened?"

He looked up and nodded.

She touched his shoulder gently. "Then why won't you accept that same forgiveness for yourself?"

Heath sighed. "I—I don't like not being in control. When Jessica died, there was nothing I could do. I already gave her my bone marrow, and that didn't do the trick. When Victoria died, I guess maybe it was easier to blame myself than realize that once again, I was powerless to do anything to stop it."

Ashlynn pulled him in for a hug. "Heath, I know you know this: Nothing we ever do is really in our control. I know you believe that in theory, but you have to truly accept it or you're going to live your entire life feeling responsible for things you can't control."

He pulled back and smiled at her. "How did you get so wise?"

She laughed as she took his hand and started walking again. His hand tightened in hers, and her chest fluttered. "You know, I did go to school for six years to study counseling. I would hope I got something out of it."

They laughed.

They got partway around the lake when Heath finally turned to her and took both her hands in his. "Ashlynn, I am sorry for keeping you at a distance. I was talking with Pastor Dustin about how sometimes we don't let our Christian friends in on our grief because we don't want to be a burden, but it's actually the opposite of what we're supposed to do. Dustin said something I haven't been able to stop thinking: about how we can't follow Jesus' command to mourn with those who mourn if they don't let us know they are mourning. I think that's what I tend to do."

"That's all I'm asking for Heath. I want to know that if you're hurting, you trust me enough to help carry your burden."

"I want that, too," Heath said. "Actually, I wanted to ask if you would do something with me?"

She looked up at him curiously. "What's that?"

"I haven't been to the cemetery to visit Victoria's grave since she died. Based on something your mom said at your dad's funeral, I get the feeling you haven't either?"

She put her head down. "No, I haven't."

"Well, then how about one way we start supporting each other is by going there now. Together."

She kept her eyes on the ground. Could she do this?

Looking back up at him, she knew her answer.

"Okay," she said. "Let's face this. Together."

As they pulled into the cemetery, Heath looked over at Ashlynn in the passenger's seat fiddling with the ring on her right ring finger. He was a little relieved she appeared to be as nervous as he was about this.

He parked his car next to where he knew Victoria's grave was located. Then, taking a deep breath, he got out of the truck and walked around to the passenger side to open Ashlynn's door.

"You ready?" he asked as she grabbed his outstretched hand.

"As ready as I think I will be."

They walked in silence the few feet to her grave. It was an ornate stone with a simple inscription: Victoria Lynn Goodman, beloved daughter and friend. On the back there was a quote from one of her favorite songs and one of her senior pictures.

"I think she would like this. It's simple but loud all at the same time. Just like Tori," he said, laughing softly.

He saw Ashlynn grimace slightly when he used her nickname.

"Hey," he said turning toward her. "I've always meant to ask you. Why does it bother you when people call her Tori? I know it's not that you don't like nicknames. People call you Ash all the time, and you seem to like it."

Ashlynn met his gaze. "When we were growing up, Victoria hated it when people called her Tori. She used to always say, 'If my parents wanted to name me Tori, they would have. My name is Victoria.' I always backed her up and corrected people when they called her Tori. Then we made the cheerleading team and people started calling her that, and when I'd try to correct them she would get mad at me. 'They're cheerleaders, and they can call me whatever they want,' she would tell me. It was kind of the start of her becoming this different person when she was around people other than me. I guess I started to think of Tori as the part of her that didn't really want me around. To me, she would always be Victoria, the girl who didn't care what other people thought about her. The girl who hated nicknames."

"I never knew that," Heath said quietly.

"Heath, I'm sorry I spent so much time in high school, and since then, blaming you for the wedge in my friendship with her. The truth is, Victoria started driving that wedge herself as soon as we were in high school. Suddenly she became concerned with popularity and what people thought about her. Meanwhile, I started going to church and met Jesus. I think as long as we didn't share that, and as long as she resented me for all the time I spent with my youth group, our friendship would always be in jeopardy."

"I didn't exactly discourage her either, though. I know I said maybe there was too much history between you and me for any kind of relationship to work, but I think I was just scared. The truth is, all the history we have, everything we've been through to get to this point? It makes us who we are."

His heart pounded, and he knew what he had to do.

He had to say it.

Now or never.

"And, Ashlynn, without all that history, I'm not sure I would have fallen in love with you."

He watched as the words sank in for her. Ashlynn gasped.

"I know it's only been a few weeks," he said, "and maybe talking about love seems too soon, but I know it's true. I love you, Ashlynn. I know it will be hard, and there are still a lot of decisions to make, but I'm willing to try a long-distance relationship if you are."

Ashlynn wiped a stray tear from her eye. "Heath, I love you, too."

Heath felt like letting out a big "whoo-hoo!" She loved him too.

"It's funny—despite all our history, or the fact that I never thought Victoria and I could have the same taste in boyfriends, I've fallen in love with you. But...."

"But?" he asked.

"But I don't think a long-distance relationship is going to work out."

His face fell, and she grabbed his hand, grinning. "I mean, how can you have a long-distance relationship in the same town?"

Same town? He couldn't process what she was saying. "You mean you decided to stay? I thought you said you were heading back to Denver next week?"

"I am heading back to Denver, but so I can wrap up everything at my old office and finish packing the rest of my things. And if the offer to rent the space next to your office still stands, then yes. I want to open a Christian counseling center and live here full time. I have a meeting with a bank in Houston on Friday to discuss financing for opening my own practice. I'll probably stay with Mom while I look for my own place and get everything set up."

Heath picked her up off her feet and twirling her around, feeling his face stretch wide in a grin.

"I take it the rental offer still stands?" she said, laughing.

He put her back on the ground, pulled her toward him, and kissed her. It was a kiss full of forgiveness, hope, and love.

Putting his hands on her shoulders, he looked deep into her eyes. "Ashlynn, I have been praying that someone would fill that spot since I moved here, and I cannot think of a better person than you."

He picked her back up, kissing her forehead.

Ashlynn suddenly looked around and started laughing.

"What's so funny?" Heath asked.

"We are twirling around and kissing in a cemetery. That cannot be how most couples get together." She laughed even harder.

"Well, dear, I think it's time we get used to the fact that we are *definitely not* most couples."

She looked up at him with a more serious look on her face. "I personally look forward to figuring out just what kind of couple we're going to be."

He pulled her in for a hug and then they walked back to his truck. He was looking forward to the same thing.

May

"So is now the appropriate time to tell you 'I told you so'?" Whitney asked Ashlynn as they finished the final food preparations for the event taking place in the next hour.

"Hey, I have dibs on that!" Isabelle said, walking in carrying two different kinds of pie.

Ashlynn sighed. "Fine. You were both right. I was running away, I had not truly forgiven Heath, I was falling for him, and I do belong in White Lake. Am I leaving out anything?"

"I think that about covers it. Can you think of anything else, Whit?" Isabelle said, smirking.

Whitney laughed. "I'm going to like having you around full-time."

"When do you officially move here, Isabelle?" Heath asked as he walked in.

"Three weeks. I'll head back to Denver on Monday and spend the next few weeks packing up all of my stuff, then drive it all here in a U-Haul."

Ashlynn smiled. Leaving her best friend and roommate had been the toughest part about deciding to move back home to White

Lake. However, a week after she'd made her decision, the music teacher at the elementary school officially announced her retirement. Isabelle decided to put in an application and was hired almost immediately. It felt great to have all the most important people in her life in one place.

Ashlynn looked over and noticed Heath staring at the calendar. "You okay over there?" she asked him quietly.

He looked over at her and smiled. "I really am. What about you? How are you feeling about the day?"

She smiled. They were a lot alike in so many ways. "Honestly, not as emotional as I thought I would be. I am finally able to look back on this day and see how far I've come in the last eleven years instead of everything I lost that day. I am, however, nervous about everything coming together for the grand opening."

Heath pulled her close and kissed her hair. "I am so glad you chose to do the dedication of your new practice on this day. It seems fitting to start a new chapter on the anniversary of the day that changed us both so much."

Ashlynn looked up at him and smiled. Once it became clear that the dedication for her new counseling practice was going to happen in May, she knew exactly the date to choose. For so long, she had let that event define her life, and it felt good to redeem it in a way. She asked Heath about it before making the final decision and he agreed.

The events of that day eleven years ago, when Victoria had died, had driven the two of them even farther apart, seemingly for good. Now, this event signified them uniting together, not only as business partners, but as a couple in love, as well. It marked a new beginning, and she was excited to see where this new journey would take her.

Or rather, where it would take them. Together.

The End

(Well, not really)

Acknowledgments

Writing and publishing a book takes a village, and this one would certainly not exist without mine. I appreciate you all more than you'll probably ever know:

Mom and Dad: Thank you for everything you've done for me. Related to this book or not. You have supported and encouraged me my entire life and I am the woman I am and the writer I am today because of you.

To my sister, Kaitlyn, and brother-in-law, Brennan: Thank you for your constant support. And thank you for letting me camp out in your guest room while I worked on edits.

To my brother, Charlie: Thank you for debating the Oxford comma with me. I'll never forget where I need it (or where you think I don't).

To Megan: Oh where to even begin. So many things to be thankful for. The brainstorm sessions. The late nights discussing our dreams (including this one!). Reading the *very* rough first draft. Letting me camp out in our sunroom for hours while writing and editing. Being the inspiration behind Ashlynn and Isabelle's friendship. This book would literally not exist without you.

To Callie: Thank you for being my first editor and encouraging me every step of the way. For lending an ear and suggestions when I was blocked. For all the prayers surrounding this dream.

To Bree and Connor: Thank you for asking for updates and being almost as excited as I am about this book release.

To Suzanne: Thank you for your feedback, and for being a fierce cheerleader.

To Michael and Kimberly: Thank you for inviting me into your family. For constantly supporting me in anyway I needed. For believing in me even when I didn't believe in myself.

To the rest of the Johnson and McElrath community groups: Thank you for the prayers, the support, and for being with me throughout this entire process.

To Dr. Jennifer and Dr. Matt: Thank you for supporting me, and for seeing me as more than just an employee but as a friend. And to you and the rest of my coworkers at Innovative Eyecare, thank you for caring about all my crazy updates and being excited to see this book come to life.

To my editor, Jessica Brodie: Thank you, thank you, thank you. Heath and Ashlynn's story is what it is because of your fabulous editing. Thank you for caring about their story almost as much as I do and making sure it was the best it could be!

To Roseanna M. White Designs for the amazing cover. It was exactly like I pictured. Seeing my name on such a beautiful cover was a dream come true.

To my beta readers: Megan, Suzanne, Tiffany, and Lauren: thank for lending your critical eye and feedback.

To Gale Nation and Holly Snead: Thank you for contributing your artwork to my funding campaign. They were the perfect compliment to the book.

To my campaign backers: Thank you, thank you, a million times thank you. This project would not exist without you. Thank you for believing in it.

And finally, thank you, Lord for this amazing opportunity. Thank you for rescuing me, for guiding me every step of the way. I pray this story brings glory to your name.

About the Author

Krystina Renae Rankin is an author who writes about love, friendship, and what it looks like to walk with God daily. She is also passionate about Christian friendship, spiritual family, and the special needs community. She is an optician by trade and honestly couldn't tell you how many pairs of glasses she owns. When she is not writing or working her day job, you can probably find her reading, watching baseball or Oklahoma City Thunder basketball, or hanging out with family and friends.

CPSIA information can be obtained
at www.ICGtesting.com
Printed in the USA
LVHW112317110921
697587LV00003B/12

CPSIA information can be obtained
at www.ICGtesting.com
Printed in the USA
LVHW112317110921
697587LV00003B/12

9 781734 571509